We Were Real

—

Nadine C. Keels

We Were Real

© 2022 by Nadine C. Keels

—

Cover Design: Nadine C. Keels

—

—

Scripture verses are indirectly quoted or paraphrased from the King James Version of *The Holy Bible*.

—

Find Nadine C. Keels online at:
www.prismaticprospects.wordpress.com

Nadine. A French name, meaning, "hope."

Nadine C. Keels is an author and blogger with a lifelong passion for the power of story. She writes the kinds of stories she wants to read but can't always find, and her aim is to spark hope and inspiration in as many people as she can reach.

—

Malt Shop Milestones Series
Vicky's Victory | Berta's Bounceback | Ari's Aria

—

Crowns Legacy Series
Reviving the Commander | Embracing the Outcast

—

Eubeltic Realm Series
Eubeltic Descent | Eubeltic Quest | Eubeltic Virtue | Eubeltic Outliers

—

Hope Beyond Series
Eminence | Simplicity

—

Movement of Crowns Series
The Movement of Crowns | The Movement of Rings | The Movement of Kings

—

For Every Love Series
Love Unfeigned | Hope Unashamed | Kiss and 'Telle?

—

Heartstrings Series
We Were Real | A Christmas So Real

—

Jhoi Series
World of the Innocent | World of Joy

—

Love by the Breather: Four Romantic Reads

Chapter One

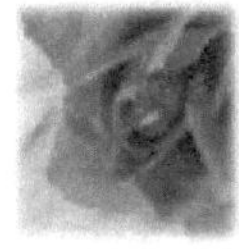

"I JUST...I MISS US, Nikki. You know?"

Here she was, traveling alone through moderate traffic this summer morning in her crossover vehicle, one with windows sufficiently tinted to keep plenty of the vehicle's contents out of outsiders' plain sight.

Driving down this street followed by that avenue, she was alone in the sense of having no real passengers with her—except for currently silent Rosa, if she counted. Wonderful as that precious girl could be for company, Rosa wasn't good for conversation en route like this, as her voice required hands-on connection for release. Not that Rosa wasn't real, but her possible status as a passenger would be an arguable point, what with her being a smooth, curvaceous, mellow creation fashioned for chords, rhythm, vibration, and soul.

A gorgeous guitar. *My manifest heartstrings.*

Yet, even if there weren't any passengers in this vehicle, simmering memories, old and new, were an almost palpable presence.

"I just...I miss us, Nikki."

Down she drove over another road paved through this place she had a hard time thinking of as her hometown. This place she'd once assumed she wouldn't return to, not even for a visit. It was technically out of her way today; she would have to be back out of town late this afternoon to head for the next county where she was booked to appear onstage at an amphitheater the following night, scheduled to perform some of her original titles, including the best from her latest independent album.

She'd balked at the idea of promoting this as a farewell tour, since she wasn't retiring. Her songwriting was still on fire, she planned to remain an active life and music vlogger, and she certainly hadn't ruled touring out of her future.

All the same, the essence of "farewell" already resided in her driving around solo like this. The members of her band had come to some crucial decisions of late. The next step they'd agreed upon for after tomorrow's last stop on this tour was possibly a breakup by another name. The possibility had been in their eyes at every recent rehearsal and concert, and she doubted those eyes would read differently once she went and met back up with the band after her day of solitary detouring.

In the meantime, she'd soon be expected at a baseball field, but just now, she was on her way to a new car dealership. A dealership at which she wouldn't be looking to buy a car.

Of course, she'd never been to the business establishment in question before. Its grand opening had been only a few months back, and she'd left this town behind her years ago. But she didn't need directions to the location, or even a reminder of the address for reference.

Barring that any drastic changes had been made to one of the roads ahead since she'd last been here, she knew exactly how to get where she was going.

A niggling bittersweetness crept over her as she handled the steering wheel, switching a specific lane here and making a specific turn there, all with the ease of muscle memory.

Hm. That part. How amazing and unsettling. To remember so easily.

One of her loose, black curls slipped down over her bronzy brow when she gave her head a slight shake. Her light gray eyes misted, and a petition came whispering through her plump, quivery lips. "My God. Please."

She had two more turns to go.

Chapter Two

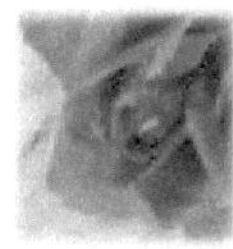

FOR THE FIRST EIGHTEEN years of her life, Nikkita Creighton had lived in this town with her parents.

There. She passed the corner that led down to her old high school, one of two secondary education institutions in this district. That school was where, during her sophomore year, she'd received a certain invitation from an upbeat, super-social classmate of hers. Jayme.

"So! Nikkita!" Jayme had called, bounding up while Nikkita was standing at her open locker in a bustling hallway. "We're having a thing at my youth group this Wednesday night. It'll be fun. Wanna come?"

Nikkita's forehead wrinkled at the unexpected invite. "A thing?" Youth group. On a Wednesday night. *Oh*. Her forehead cleared. "You mean a church service."

"Well, yeahhh," Jayme admitted with a nod toward one shrugging shoulder, her strawberry-blond messy bun bouncing high on her head. "But it's not like on Sundays with all the adults. They're in their quiet little Bible study classes on Wednesdays, but we let loose in youth group."

"Let loose? How loose?" Nikkita glanced down at her dark pair of flared jeans complementing the fairly ample hips of her pear figure. "Would I have to wear a dress?"

"No, youth group is nice and casual. Me and my mom can pick you up. Wait—you don't drive yet, do you?"

"Yes and no. Got my learner's permit."

"I figured. Me too. So we'll give you a ride. Wanna come?"

"Um, don't know." Nikkita almost shook her head, rummaging around in her locker for her math book. "Does letting loose mean there won't be a sermon to sit through?"

"Aww, come on," Jayme urged, lifting her arm that was free of textbooks and reaching out to take an imploring hold of Nikkita's elbow for a second. "The message won't be boring or anything, I promise. Our youth pastor, Pastor Tyler—he's awesome. Like, *really* awesome. The youth praise team is great too, and I know you like music 'cause the talent show." She whipped her hand out to the side, palm upward. "So! Wanna come?"

Yes, Nikkita had picked a song and sung her grieving teenage heart out of the tender lyrics while standing in the spotlight of her school's talent show earlier that year. She'd been the finale of the program and earned a standing ovation followed by a whirlwind week of sudden popularity before she faded back to the outskirts of most of her schoolmates' attention.

Something told her that whatever music they'd "let loose" to at Jayme's church wouldn't quite match any kind of music Nikkita was truly into.

She wasn't unaccustomed to being the odd girl out on one level or another, though. Unlike seemingly all the other girls she knew, Nikkita hated talking on the phone. She spent far more time seriously immersed in music than she spent watching TV or hanging out at the mall. She only went to parties that were family related: out-of-town get-togethers where she could cut up with her generation of cousins, most of whom were still alive. And going to school in this rather homogenous area, she was used to being one of only one or two brown-skinned kids in her proximity on most days.

It would probably be the same way at Jayme's youth group. But Jayme was friendly enough, and it felt pretty nice to be singled out and invited somewhere.

Nikkita decided she might as well be game. "Okay, sure. Thanks. I'll go."

"Yes!" That earned a grin from Jayme. "It'll be great! They're gonna have pri—"

Cut off by the warning bell for the upcoming start of classes, Jayme bid Nikkita a rushed goodbye for now and scampered off.

That Wednesday evening, it didn't take Nikkita long to gain a better understanding of what she'd agreed to. Jayme's mom did indeed swing by Nikkita's house to pick her up, but Jayme herself wasn't in the minivan filled with five other girls, two of the others also students from Nikkita's school. It turned out that Jayme was riding to the church with her dad and another carful of passengers that had to go in a different direction to make the rest of the pick-ups.

"Outreach Nite!" a fluorescent banner above the closed sanctuary doors enthused as Nikkita stepped from outside and into the church foyer with Jayme's pack of invitees. While standing in the growing crowd of teenagers milling around as they waited for the sanctuary doors to open, Nikkita pieced together the nature of the event through snatches of laughter and chitchat as Jayme made introductions.

On this particular night, the three youth group members who brought the most first-time visitors to church would be the big winners.

"Three prize boxes full of goodies! Maybe some gift cards," Jayme gushed in the foyer, having done her part in rounding up and bringing in a bunch of young souls who were unchurched, apparently as far as she could tell. "Maybe there'll be enough eatable stuff in the box to divvy it up with our team if I—if we win."

"Ah. Maybe." Nikkita was on a team, then. *Go, team.* She went with the flow in the foyer for a while, being included in a round of introductions that felt more like an exhibition.

"And look! I even outreached to get this one to come, and she's Black. Beat *that.*"

Well, no, that wasn't what Jayme said as she placed a presenting hand on Nikkita's shoulder. What Jayme did say to everyone, in a loud, perfectly overpronounced manner she hadn't used for her other guests, was "And this is one more I brought! *Her* name is *Ni-KEET-ta.*"

Heat had begun to rise in Nikkita's cheeks.

That introduction got a small shake of the head from one of Jayme's listeners: a brown-haired guy with sandy-toned skin and a husky build. His hands were parked in the pockets of his jeans, and the essence of an apology shone in his dark eyes as they met Nikkita's.

She took a step back. A break was in order. She asked Jayme where the nearest restroom was.

Minutes later, on her trip down the hall and around a corner, away from the noisy foyer, Nikkita toyed with the idea of wandering around the building for the rest of the evening, but she paused when her hearing was met by the rise and fall of faint chords from piano keys.

She followed the sound and soon found the open doors of a chapel room. "Pre-Service Prayer" the sign beside the doorway read. The smattering of people inside, all adults, were spread about in different rows of cushioned chairs under the room's softly dimmed lights. A couple of the chapel's occupants were kneeling at their seats, but the others were sitting, most of them with bowed heads. Up on the room's dais before the chapel's front wall of large windows stood a piano, where a woman sat playing, the look on her upturned face beatific even with her eyes closed and no smile on her lips.

Nikkita was familiar with a general sound to traditional hymns, and she'd bet her bi-weekly allowance (but not in church, of course) that the peaceful chords of a hymn were what she heard now, a song embellished with apparent improvisation by the enraptured woman at the keys.

Slipping into the room, Nikkita chose a chair near a wall where she could stare toward the evening's fading light glowing through the windows. In the midst of pre-service prayer, she simply sat there.

But she didn't simply sit. It was a natural habit of Nikkita's to allow music—all that was within, beneath, and around it—to speak to her. Hence, she kept her gaze toward the windows and sat waiting. Listening. Wondering. Seeking. Absorbing. Sensing.

And...knowing?

Was that what this was, this subtle but distinctly different stirring that had begun at her very core, something she couldn't recall feeling in this way before? Could she be wondering something while somehow knowing it all at once?

In time, the music drifted to a close. The room remained still, the air bearing no sound but occasional whispers of lingering prayer lifting into the atmosphere.

It wasn't until the others in the room began to rise and make their way out of the chapel, likely heading to their Bible study classes, that Nikkita became fully aware of the warm drop that had slipped through her lower lashes to make a trail down her face, clear to her chin.

She didn't end up wandering around for the rest of the evening. She went and met up with Jayme's "team" in the sanctuary and respected the rocking music and joyous singing in the room for what it was, though she didn't jump around or throw her hands in the air as many of the others did. The youth pastor who eventually ran up to the platform with a cordless mic looked to be somewhere in his thirties. Whatever he said in his sermon might have been awesome in accordance with Jayme's recommendation, but Nikkita couldn't tell either way.

Her mind had stolen away from the room, going back to wait, to wonder, and to rest in the church's chapel.

It took the shifting of gears near the end of the service to reclaim her attention. The band began playing a slow song, and Pastor Tyler was saying, "Those of you who know me know that my heart is to see you healed. Healed and thriving. Too many adults think that young people these days don't go through anything real. I guess a lot of adults in every generation feel that way, but unfortunately, it's either due to their forgetfulness, ignorance, or arrogance. Fear, stress, heartbreak, tragedy—those things don't have an age minimum attached. God doesn't discount what you feel and go through just because you're young.

"If any of you want prayer for healing tonight, you're welcome to come forward. Our altar workers are here for you..."

Some of the service's attendees left their seats to go up and stand before the platform, Jayme accompanying two of her guests up there. While Nikkita watched as those identified as altar workers began listening to people's prayer requests and placing their hands on people's shoulders to pray for them, no urge to join them came over Nikkita. So she remained at her seat. Thinking about the chapel.

"So! Nikkita! Wasn't it great?" Jayme wanted to know after the service was over, as she was pocketing her restaurant and department store gift cards and passing out some packs of her prize box's candy to the bunch of young souls who'd won her a share of the night's honors.

Nikkita's head moved vaguely up and down as a pack of sweet 'n' sour gumdrops slapped down into her hand. "Actually, yes. I think so."

Her answer got a gratified squeal out of Jayme, who couldn't know what her first-time visitor was really referring to.

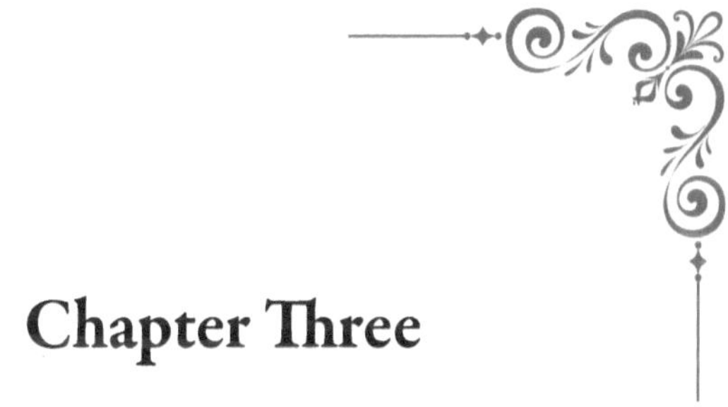

Chapter Three

"WELL. IT COULD BE A good opportunity to make friends" and "Being involved in something like that will be a plus on your academic résumé when you start applying to colleges" were the main positive but slow responses from Nikkita's mom and dad after she told them over dinner one evening that she was joining the youth choir at church. Those slow responses followed the married Creighton couple's initial confusion, given that their daughter had only visited the church twice.

"All right, now," Nikkita's dad spoke again from his place at the dinner table, a questioning line between his eyebrows as he started unpeeling a banana, "what led to this decision, again?"

Nikkita had never understood her dad's affinity for eating bananas with anything, even meatloaf and mashed potatoes. She shrugged, setting her fork down on her half-full plate. "Trying something new. It'd be more interesting than only going to sit in church services, I think. And I wouldn't have to carry as much weight in the choir as I would on the smaller, um, praise team, they call it."

She left it at that for fear of sounding strange. Though she would have liked to give her parents a better explanation, she didn't have the words to clarify what was drawing her to do this.

Perhaps if her parents had been there and felt it. In the chapel...

It wasn't long before Nikkita was making her regular way to church for Sunday morning services, Wednesday night youth group, and youth choir practices every other Saturday afternoon. She was grateful for the cooperation of her parents who took turns riding down there with her while she still only had her learner's permit. Once she earned her driver's license, she started borrowing her mom's car to make her way to church by herself.

"So! Nikkita! I'm so glad that, like, out of everybody I asked, you stuck," Jayme rejoiced at one point, her words giving Nikkita a quick visual of a cook testing the readiness of long, boiled noodles by tossing some of the strings against a wall. "Good thing I invited you that day, huh? High-five to Pastor Tyler for coming up with the outreach idea in the first place. Totally a God thing."

Jayme tilted her head, her gaze veering off and her next comment riding a dreamy sigh floating from her mouth. "But, hey. He's so awesome."

Nikkita smiled a bit, nearly replying with a melodic line from a song they sometimes sang in youth group about the awesomeness of God. But she paused, realizing she couldn't tell which "he" Jayme was talking about just then.

Except for special occasions such as the church's annual Christmas and Holy Week programs, the youth choir's schedule was to sing one song a month for services, once on a Wednesday and a repeat the following Sunday. While the various pieces of contemporary music arranged for the choir weren't necessarily pieces Nikkita would choose to listen to as an individual, singing those arrangements with a group under the guidance of a professionally trained director, Minister Kate, was a learning experience for Nikkita.

Still, what she looked forward to most were pre-service times in the chapel on Sundays and Wednesdays, and also the opening of choir practice on Saturdays. Minister Kate would turn on soft music over the sanctuary's sound system while the choir members spread out to different spots and corners of the room to spend some time in personal prayer. Nikkita would go and sit on the floor in relative privacy around the corner of the sound booth, resting back against the booth's wall.

Listening and wondering. Seeking and finding. Absorbed in encounters she couldn't describe, and never feeling in those moments that her inability to describe them mattered.

Pastor Tyler, who was often working in his office at the church on Saturdays, would come visit the sanctuary during some of those times, stopping to check on choir members here and there, joining different ones in prayer. On one occasion, the first time he came and found Nikkita sitting on the other side of the sound booth, she was initially startled, reaching up with one sleeve of her zip-up hoodie to dry the dampness from under her eyes.

"I'm sorry, Nikkita," Pastor Tyler murmured, crouching down a few feet away from her. "Didn't mean to make you jump."

"It's all right." Nikkita sniffled, wanting to get her compact mirror out of her purse beside her so that she could check on her mascara, but she didn't.

Pastor Tyler opened his hands. "Would you like me to pray with you for a sec?"

"Um, sure." Nikkita dabbed under her eyes again with the cuff of her sleeve. "That'd be fine."

"Okay." After Pastor Tyler bowed his head and sent up a brief petition concerning Nikkita's home, her school, and her wellbeing, she thanked him, but he said with a mild smile, "Thank *Him* as He works in your life and heals whatever aches you carry in your heart. He sees you as what you are: a pearl of great price, worthy of care and safekeeping. Remember that."

Nikkita said nothing more as Pastor Tyler stood back up and moved on. Because stopping by was something he did with other members of the youth choir, it didn't mean he'd singled her out, exactly. It still felt something like it, though, and the feeling was pretty nice.

Nikkita continued praying on her own until it was time for the choir to rehearse.

However, even as she was settling into her routine of involvement at church, she could tell that her participation in the choir didn't bring her the same level of fun that it did for most of the other teens around her. She soon gathered that besides the few random faces that sometimes popped up and then quit the youth choir about as quickly as they had joined, the choir's members had been doing church together their whole lives, basically. It wasn't the kind of bond that a newcomer could slide right into without having been there for the shared history.

Within the sociable, electric environment that made up the choir and the church's youth group in general—along with regular high-fives and jaunty greetings and blessings from a Pastor Tyler who knew Nikkita by name, and Jayme's brand of bouncy partiality for the outreach guest of hers who'd wound up sticking—Nikkita experienced the reality of being present but not being as "in the mix" as those who'd been "in" from jump.

Odd girl out. Again. She gave a small, resigned laugh at the thought, once. It wasn't anyone's fault. People fit where they fit, didn't where they didn't. After about three and a half months of church services and choir membership, it was already hard for Nikkita to imagine she'd find a much better fit in that environment than the reasonable one she had.

She might have gone on, continuing not to imagine it, if not for one unusual Saturday she couldn't have anticipated.

A Saturday that changed some sort of everything.

Chapter Four

"MINSTER KATE? HI. UM, I'll have to miss choir practice this Saturday," Nikkita said on a Wednesday night after the end of youth service and Bible study classes, as she'd gotten a hold of the choir director in a hallway that seemed otherwise empty.

Wait. Breathe. Keep it together. Nikkita had to take a breath before explaining. "My mom broke her leg and is mostly out of commission for a while, but my dad's going up to Greyridge on Saturday for a procedure. He can't drive himself home afterwards, so I'm going along."

After Minister Kate gave a ready excusal and spoke a blessing for her dad, Nikkita thanked her and turned around, seeing a shadow disappear from around the corner of the hallway some feet away from her. The hallway must not have been as empty as she'd thought.

In a waiting room at Greyridge Hospital that Saturday afternoon, Nikkita was doing a poor job of distracting herself with the biology homework lying in her lap. She envied the waiting room's one other occupant: a woman curled up and taking a nap on the couch across the way from Nikkita's chair.

How could anyone manage to look so relaxed and cozy in this place?

As Nikkita sat trying to decide whether or not she was ready to give up on her sham of a study session, her peripheral vision detected movement at the waiting room entrance. She turned her head in that direction, her eyes widening as she did so.

There, with the sides of his jacket hiked up a tad where his hands were parked in the pockets of his jeans, stood the husky guy with dark eyes Nikkita had half-met on her first Wednesday night at church. A guy who was also a member of the youth choir.

Nikkita had to do some shuffling around in her mind to make sure she'd say the right name. "Ian?"

A tentative smile lit his face, as if hearing her correct identification relieved him. "Hey, Nikkita."

"Hey." She glanced over at the sleeping woman on the couch before looking back at Ian. "You waiting for someone here too?"

"No. Yeah." He brought a hand out of his pocket and indicated Nikkita. "Actually, I came here to see if you wanted company."

"Me?" Nikkita's eyes hadn't gone back to their normal size. Her mind did some more shuffling. "You knew I'd be at the hospital?"

Ian's head tipped in a half-nod of confession. "I was on my way to get a drink of water at church on Wednesday, overheard you tell Minister Kate. Sounded like you'd be here waiting by yourself." When Nikkita made no reply to that, he asked, "Is it all right that I'm here? I know medical stuff is private."

"How did you...?" A wrinkle came to Nikkita's brow. "You knew what name to ask for at the desk?"

"Yeah. No. Well, I had to guess that your dad's name is 'Creighton' too." Ian paused as Nikkita went speechless, and his smile became somewhat more definite. "Yes, I know your last name, Nikkita Creighton. We're on the same list of choir members." The first two fingers of his free hand came out, pointing up toward his eyes and then toward Nikkita's for a second. "I pay attention."

Nikkita budged forward in her chair, trying to make sense of this unexpected twist in her present situation. "So you skipped practice to come to the hospital," she stated and asked at the same time, nearly adding "for me" to the end of her inquiring comment but shying away from the words.

There was caution in the lowering of Ian's voice. "When you talked to Minister Kate about it, you sounded all shaky."

Although Nikkita couldn't recall that specific detail for herself, she didn't doubt that it was true, the mention of it sending a telltale tremble through her insides. She reached into the chair beside her, removing the backpack she'd set there and leaning to push it under her seat, waving Ian over from his place of limbo in the waiting room entrance.

As he came and took the cleared seat beside her, Nikkita admitted, "It feels silly to be this nervous here." She closed her biology book over the couple of homework sheets inside of it. "My dad's surgery isn't a major one."

Ian shrugged. "But it's surgery. And these places aren't famous for giving off the most, um"—he gave his hands a quick, stiff shake—"feel-good vibes. If I can say that."

Ian's hands came down to brace themselves on top of his generous thighs, and he kept his face turned to Nikkita, giving her the opportunity to consider him. Even apart from his build, there wasn't much to call "small" about the guy. His eyes were large, his lips full, and even his hair, which he wore a little long on top, was thick, as if his follicles had decided that a lack of volume wouldn't do justice to his make-up. What he didn't have the greatest abundance of were his freckles, as they mostly graced only his nose and upper cheeks, but they still made their presence known.

Hmm.

Out of everything that could have been the case right now, he, of all people, was here, of all places. He had to be interested enough to know what the deal was with Nikkita, so she decided it'd be all right to give him an explanation. A condensed version, at least.

She swallowed before beginning. "I'm real close to my cousins on both sides of my family. None of them live around here, but still. We're tight." An inevitable prickling started up in her eyes, and she blinked at it, falling short of blinking it away. "I lost my cousin Renée in a hospital, earlier this year. This school year." Her voice dropped with a shudder. "Failed surgery after a car accident."

Ian hadn't been smiling, but his face still fell, the braced position of his hands slackening. "Oh, man. I'm sorry," he said, his murmur of sympathy unaccompanied by shock. He inclined his shaking head toward his own piece to share. "I lost my dad in a hospital. Last year. Complications after a heart attack."

The prickling in Nikkita's eyes seared, bringing a blur to her vision until dampness escaped. "Oh…" Her hand came up, almost reaching for Ian's arm but instead lifting to hover near her mouth.

Ian did some rapid blinking himself, clearing his throat. "Not that your dad isn't going to be fine. You know?" He darted his eyes around and got up from his seat, stepping over to the table on the other side of Nikkita's chair. "I didn't come to turn this into a vigil."

It didn't make much difference that the box of tissue he swiped up from the table and held out to Nikkita had already been within her reach. She snatched two tissues out of the box with a short chortle of gratitude. "No you didn't, apparently," she confirmed, and as he sat back down with the box, she swept her gaze over him, one side of her mouth curving upward. "Doesn't look like you brought any candles along."

"What? Aw, I've got some in my car." Ian set the box down on his thigh. "But those are for emergencies on the road. Like if my headlights fall out one night and I run over 'em."

An effervescent, involuntary snort burst from Nikkita. She folded her tissues and dabbed them under her eyes. "Mascara running?"

Ian's eyebrows inched closer together. "For president?"

"No," Nikkita deadpanned less than a beat after him, lowering her tissues. "Behind."

It took a second for Ian's bulb to click on at that, and he pointed at her. "Ah!" he said with an appreciative snicker. After she snickered with him, he gave her face a look-over, telling her, "You're fine."

What with the lingering appreciation in Ian's small smile, Nikkita missed a beat before nodding her thanks to him, still brushing two fingertips over her cheeks in case of any possible clinging tissue bits he might not have thought warranted a mention.

Once she was sufficiently sure she was together, Nikkita let her reasoning return to the novelty this situation held for her. "We've barely talked before," she mused aloud to Ian. "But you came here."

Ian's look turned sheepish. "Risking the possibility that you'd think it was stalkerish, yeah." He laughed, spreading his hands. "It's okay to maybe walk up to a girl you don't know in the library or something, and ask to share a study table. Asking a girl to a movie or to go out and get a soda before you've ever said more than 'hi' to her—that can be borderline. But coming right out and asking the new girl..." He let his jaw hang to accommodate a wide, exaggerated smile as his hands collaborated to wag two fingers in circles toward Nikkita. "'So, hey, how about a meet-up in a ward of the hospital this weekend, you and me?'" He then tossed that exaggeration aside. "I thought it might be at least a little less weird to just show up here and risk you kicking me out."

Nikkita chewed on that before she raised her fingers to do some noncommittal wagging back, her tissues still in hand. "I wouldn't kick you out." She nodded toward the waiting room entrance. "I'd call security and have them kick you out."

Ian seemed grateful for the droll smile she extended to him with that comment. The two of them fell quiet for a moment, and his train shifted tracks. "Speaking of weird... I always felt kinda bad about the weird way things got started, that first night."

He paused long enough for Nikkita to follow his shift. She didn't need him to specify the incident. *Oh. That.* She drew a breath in with her nose, pursing her lips.

Ian's shoulders came slightly up and in as if to hunch down over the words. "I've known Jayme since kindergarten. She's good people, but I don't think she...was listening to herself, that day. I thought it was pretty messed up." Nikkita didn't answer, and Ian sat up straighter, holding up his hands. "Sorry if it's embarrassing to bring it up."

Yes. It had been embarrassing, for one thing, but Nikkita didn't think of it as his to atone for. She let the memory slither over her and chose a calm reply. "I can't say if she was listening to herself or not." She gave Ian a direct, steady look. "But it helps to know that you were."

Yielded to the hold of Nikkita's stare, Ian nodded, leaving the last word about the incident to her.

She was then free to be the one to nudge the two of them in another direction. "And to make sure I was listening to you—" Nikkita worked disbelief into the smile she gave him. "Asking a girl out for a soda?"

That reference livened Ian right up. "Oh, you know. Not getting a can or a bottle of pop, something you can grab out of a vending machine or whatever. But going out to get a soda."

Nikkita's mask of disbelief stayed put.

"A real one," Ian clarified, holding up an imaginary glass for presentation. Or evidence. "At a soda fountain," he added, the strength of his presentation wavering.

Nikkita quirked an eyebrow at him.

Ian's next words of description slid out with slowed momentum. "Like at a lunch counter. In a drugstore."

Nikkita's eyes squinted, her smile growing. "What century are you living in?"

Giving a laugh, Ian upheld his glass with renewed conviction. "Soda fountains *are* from this century," he asserted in his own defense. "I first saw it on *Leave It to Beaver.*"

"Oh, right, right." Nikkita let both of her brows pop upward. "Nice, modern stuff. Just before the invention of color TV. And the internet."

If more laughter tried to get away from Ian, he suppressed it, perhaps unable to stop the way it played about his lips. "There's a *Beaver* episode where the parents, Ward and June, sit at a drugstore counter and ask the soda fountain guy for two black and whites. Had to ask my mom what those are. Soda—uh, seltzer—added to vanilla ice cream and chocolate syrup. It sounds good." He hesitated, a change coming to his tone as if he recognized a question slipping into his next phrase before he voiced it. "Black and white."

Nikkita studied him, checking her sense to work out what she'd heard. "Yes, it does," she agreed with him about the sound of the soda, taking a moment, then nodding in acceptance of his question.

Or at least what his question could have been, whether wholly or in part.

"And yes. I am," Nikkita said, bringing a fingertip up close to one of her light eyes. "My mom's peepers." She reached over to coil one of her dark curls around her finger. "My dad's hair. Even though he cuts his shorter." She let go of her curl and turned her hand, holding the back of it forward, alongside her face. "My dad's mom's skin. Same shade."

Ian's eyelids dropped a responsive degree as he watched her.

Nikkita poked her finger in a dimple she didn't have. "A lot of people didn't learn that my beige parents are biracial until after the two of them produced a brown kid."

Nikkita's remark was matter-of-fact. Ian's reception wasn't. His gaze didn't move from her. "Amazing how that works sometimes," he murmured, a faint rasp in his throat, a soft spark in his eyes.

Nikkita stared back at him, his murmur dropping through her placid surface like a smooth stone, sending a stirring ripple through her.

It was Ian's second time clearing his throat. "The power of DNA," he qualified his previous observation, stopping to think about it. "Or genes," he corrected himself, appearing unsure if his correction was correct.

An entertained tilt came to Nikkita's head.

"Or...chromosomes," Ian reached, dragging out the syllables, giving up, his resulting smile a lopsided one.

"Uh huh." Nikkita picked up her biology book from her lap, holding it over to him. "Sounds like you need to brush up."

Ian threw up blocking hands, recoiling from the textbook as if she'd fished it out of a muddy bucket of poison. "I prefer to save weekend homework for Monday mornings while I'm scarfing down my cereal."

Nikkita plopped the book back down in her lap. "Slacker."

"Nah. Daredevil." When Nikkita gave him a withering look, Ian lifted an authoritative finger in the air. "Unless you know the thrill of racing against the clock to cram three-hours' worth of homework into the last possible fifteen minutes, don't knock it."

His comeback got a grin out of Nikkita. "My fault."

Ian grinned at her in return and let that topic go, retrieving his invisible glass and raising it to her. "So, um, I'm sure you've guessed I'm just vanilla."

"Hm? Hmm." With little concern for his glass or anything that might spill out of it, Nikkita took a light hold of Ian's wrist and turned his hand to examine the back of it before holding it up next to his face, telling him, "More like French vanilla. Shade wise." She then released his wrist and pointed toward his nose. "French vanilla *bean*," she elaborated, her fingertip dotting the air several quick times toward his spread of freckles.

As an amused, pleased aspect came and settled over Ian's features, Nikkita inserted a disclaimer. "Not that we can always guess the right ingredients by looking. As we know."

Ian nodded, taking that into account. "Dutch vanilla bean then," he pronounced, "if we're talking ingredients. Don't know if there's any ice cream flavor called that, though."

"Well." Nikkita tapped a finger to her chin. "There's Dutch chocolate."

Ian took that as a chance for another question. "You?"

Nikkita mouthed a smiling "no," her head going from side to side. "Spanish in me. And Irish, even though I hardly ever wear green."

Ian lifted one of his feet for a second, spotlighting his large sneaker. "I hardly ever wear clogs. Go figure."

Nikkita reflected on that foot of his. "Do you speed skate?" she asked on a good-humored impulse. When Ian showed a hint of surprise that she'd thought to ask that question, she told him, "The Summer Olympics are better, but I watch the Winter Games too."

He then looked at her as if she'd shot her marbles straight and true but lost them just that fast. "Winter Olympics are better," he said.

"Nope." Nikkita didn't give his opposing opinion an inch. "Track, gymnastics, and swimming, all the way. All day."

"Nah. The adrenaline rush isn't the realest unless a sport is zooming vertically down packed snow on an actual mountain or flying at breakneck speed over a hard sheet of ice."

Sidestepping any need to counter that, Nikkita pressed him with, "So you skate?"

After acting as if he were going to give a nod for the most foregone conclusion in the world, Ian grunted instead. "On wheels," he owned up but did so as a declaration. "When youth group goes down to the rink. Other than that, baseball season's started at school, and I play first base. But that's beside the point."

"Ah. Okay. School athlete," Nikkita said, letting him off the winter sports hook. "What grade?"

"I'm a sophomore."

"Oh, yeah. Me too." Giving in to an automatic suspicion of hers, Nikkita asked him, "Do you wear a letterman's jacket?"

Ian sputtered like an All-American varsity type exposed. "I...have one," he allowed with comically widened eyes. "I don't wear it that much."

Nikkita gave her eyelashes a teasing flutter. "Only when you're about to take a girl out to the soda fountain."

Ian took the bait with an affected air of dignity. "They wear letterman *sweaters* on *Leave It to Beaver*." He popped the collar of the jacket he currently had on, which had no varsity ties whatsoever. "I'm much more modern than that."

Nikkita smirked at him. "Much more modern than this century."

Ian's forehead creased at the sound of that trap. He got a wobbly hold on a smirk of his own. "Uh, sure."

Whipping her face away from him, Nikkita spurted with spirited laughter, trying to keep her voice down on account of the woman across the way who was yet curled up in a nap. Once Nikkita had herself under control, she turned to Ian, pointing back and forth between him and herself. "Anyway. I guess I haven't been paying as much attention as you have."

It didn't take Ian long to catch her meaning. He answered it with an overstatement. "Your way of saying even though I've noticed you at church, you haven't noticed me, and therefore I'm unnoticeable." He flopped back in his chair, upsetting the box of tissue on his leg, making it teeter toward the floor. "Woe is me. Oh, the pain," he lamented, bringing the back of one fist up to his brow. "The agony."

Nikkita snatched up and saved the tissue box right before it would have met a tumbling fate. "The drama," she retorted, holding the box Ian's way. "I got your name right when you walked in here, didn't I?"

He seized a tissue out of the box, whisking it over a nonexistent river of tears. "You were only guessing."

Nikkita laughed in acknowledgment. "It was an educated guess. Like you said, I'm the new girl at church. You've had one new face hanging around the place to learn and put a name to. I've had a whole crowd of you to learn."

Ian peered up at her, his head bobbing with a theatrical, dry sniffle. "I'll give you that."

"You better, 'cause it isn't like I haven't noticed you at all." The memory of a shaking head with a dark-eyed apology in a group of teenagers flashed across Nikkita's mind while Ian sat back up in his chair, a curious and hopeful look having come to his face.

The look, showing up on the tails of his theatrical act, appeared to be only half joking.

Nikkita set the box of tissue down on her biology book. Although she didn't necessarily want or intend to take her statement back, she still felt it best to make her initial aim clear. "I was going to say you'll have to fill me in on your last name."

Her clarification didn't appear to disappoint Ian. "Everson."

"Everson." Letting the surname introduce itself to her imagination, she began gently rocking in her seat, opening her mouth to sing. "Ian Evvv-ver-son hummm-ble, there's noo-o place..." When Ian eyed her as if she'd shot and lost an additional marble or two, Nikkita smiled, wrinkling her nose. "Finishing that wouldn't make sense, huh?"

Ian snickered. "Didn't make sense when you started it either." He calmed himself, his countenance opening with another look of appreciation. "Real pretty voice makes up for it, though."

Nikkita's nose unwrinkled itself, a trace of her smile remaining as it changed.

"Sounds like you could sing some solos if you wanted," Ian suggested to her, "unlike most of us amateurs in the choir. You should try out for one."

Warmth had risen in Nikkita's cheeks. "The new girl's still pretty new for that."

With a shrug, Ian told her, "Then sing to the Lord a new song, new girl." His gaze kept an encouraging hold on hers, and Nikkita's hesitant smile grew in spite of itself.

Earlier, it had seemed to her that her time in this room would drag by, in the midst of unreasonable envy for a napping woman who was likely exhausted and could be waiting for someone having surgery for a frightening health concern. But once Nikkita and Ian were on their feet later, it amazed her that the time hadn't felt longer. A nurse had stepped into the room to inform Nikkita that her dad's procedure was over, and as Ian was set to take his leave, Nikkita stopped him with a hand on his arm.

"Thank you for coming here, Ian. For real. Wasn't stalkerish of you. This was a nice surprise."

Ian's eyes shone in light of his afternoon exchange with her. All of it. "It's what I'd want someone to do for me, if I had to be here." He ducked his head toward her to add, "And it's cool to see you, anyway."

Indecision made Nikkita's hand linger a moment longer than she would've planned, had she planned this. If she'd known Ian better, she would've demonstrated more. As it was, she refrained from doing so, even being fully aware of how much she wanted to.

No matter that the two of them had barely said more than "hi" to each other before this afternoon meet-up, of sorts, in a ward of the hospital.

Chapter Five

FOLLOWING THE FIRST solo she sang in church, Nikkita went from being the odd girl out to being a girl who stood out. A girl who stood out for something besides her "new girl" status and her skin color.

It took her longer than usual to get back home on the night the whole youth group first heard her, what with all the attention she got after the service.

"Isn't she something?" Jayme kept asking her friends as she stood beside Nikkita in the foyer, taking half a dozen chances to hug the shoulders and waist of the youth choir's soloist of the night. "From a school stage to actual ministry. Look at that! Look what God is doing."

In response to that prompting from Jayme, Nikkita looked over and through the activity in the foyer. The room was filled with keyed-up teens along with bustling grownups rounding up younger kids fresh out of the children's Bible classes, and near the church's front doors with a couple of his guy friends stood Ian, his hands in their usual parking spaces and a smile in the eyes he had trained on Nikkita.

"Yeah," Nikkita murmured, her eyelids lowering and rising in a thoughtful blink. "Look at that."

Ian wasn't going to come over and gush about what was practically her church debut, she knew. He'd soon be driving his mom and middle-school-aged sister home, and he would instant message Nikkita later. The two of them had been IMing each other on the computer almost every day since the day he'd come to keep her company at Greyridge.

"Can I have your number?" he'd asked Nikkita while walking her out to her mom's car the next day after the morning service at church. When she'd hesitated, he'd hurried to switch up his question. "Do you IM?"

Oh, yes. Nikkita IMed all the time, usually with her cousins. Yes, it was okay that Ian had asked for her number; she just didn't like talking on the phone, that was all. Yes, Ian could IM her if he wanted. That'd be nice.

Yes. Look at that.

Nikkita's eyes now returned Ian's smile from across the busy foyer, extending the moment before she'd have to go back to the awkward work of responding to the compliments being directed her way.

Was it appropriate to reply with thanks when people praised you for your singing in church? Or were you supposed to redirect the glory with a "Praise God" or something similar?

In response to an interested question from a girl named Sandra, Jayme wound up drawing her group of listeners away with an animated story of how she'd been the one to discover

Nikkita at their school's talent show, and Pastor Tyler appeared from around Nikkita's side.

He high-fived her. "Way to go tonight, Nikkita! That was beautiful." He grinned. "What did I tell you? Such a pearl. What a gift, and to see you giving yourself back to Him that way. Genuine and mature. Using your talent to bless Him."

There. Now that would be a wrong place to say "thank you," right? Pastor Tyler would probably reply with a "thank *Him*" instead, wouldn't he?

Nikkita hadn't decided what her response would be before Pastor Tyler brought a hand up to his chest, giving his head a faint shake, his grin softening with his next comment. "His heart must have melted for you, then and there. It had to."

Nikkita nearly replied to that, but paused.

Pastor Tyler removed his hand from his chest to give her another high-five and a jaunty "Have a good day at school tomorrow!" before he moved on to greet others in the foyer, and Jayme returned with a bounce.

"So! Nikkita! Me and Sandra started feeling snacky at the same time, so a bunch of us are making a quick run to the store. Wanna come?"

Nikkita said yes and went along on the group snack run, her imagination mulling over the concept of a heart melting in someone's chest.

While nothing out of the ordinary would happen whenever Nikkita's mom and dad would see her sit down with her schoolbooks or an occasional novel around the house, her parents started giving her odd looks when they'd see her reading a Bible in the living room or at the kitchen table. A Bible she'd recently saved up some allowance to purchase.

Unsure if she might be sensing skepticism or disapproval from her parents, Nikkita didn't talk about the Bible with them. She still knew that words would fail her if she tried to describe what she experienced when she prayed. And despite a few invitations from their daughter, the Creighton couple didn't make a regular habit of attending church with Nikkita.

Still, they did come to church to hear her when she sang her first Sunday morning solo. In the foyer after the service, her parents had the chance to meet Minster Kate: "It's been a joy to have your daughter singing with us these past months. Such a voice."

To meet Pastor Tyler: "Nikkita is on the ball, already showing such dedication to our youth ministry. That kind of maturity is wonderful to see."

To meet Jayme: "Awesome how it only took inviting her here with me once, and she came and stuck. Now that she's in the choir, she's even more involved in youth group than I am! Technically."

The church's senior pastor, Pastor Paul, and his wife also greeted Nikkita in the foyer that day. She hadn't talked to the head of the church before, hadn't seen him much anyplace besides the pulpit on Sundays. Due to the way he and his wife initially appeared confused when Nikkita made her introductions, she suspected they'd been expecting that this morning's stand-out soloist from the youth choir would have browner-skinned parents than the Creighton couple she presented.

Then, as a part of her wondered if she'd done some intentional saving for last, Nikkita got to introduce Ian to her parents.

After initial pleasantries, Ian pointed between Nikkita and himself. "I knew right away we'd be friends 'cause she got my jokes," he informed Mr. and Mrs. Creighton.

Nikkita had told her mom and dad weeks ago about Ian coming to wait with her at the hospital. He didn't specifically mention it now, didn't paint any pictures of Super Everson flying up to Greyridge and swooping in to the rescue or anything.

"Gave as good as I got," Nikkita added to the account, leaning forward to fake-whisper over to her parents, "which wasn't that hard."

Ian turned to her, narrowing his eyes. "You're saying I tell bad jokes?"

Nikkita smiled up at him, reaching to link her arm through his. "Miserable."

"Huh." Ian lifted and dropped a shoulder. "So you crack up at miserable jokes, then."

"Oh, dear dude." Nikkita squeezed his arm. "Those are charity crack-ups."

"Ah, well. That's cool. Faith, hope, and charity. I'll take all of 'em, thanks."

"Yeah? Now you sound like somebody over-ordering from a menu."

Ian finally met her smile with one of his own. "At the lunch counter?"

Nikkita conceded with a laugh. "In a drugstore."

She then noticed her dad looking on as if the two young folks before him had gone bananas, but he wasn't sure how to react, given his feelings about that tropical fruit. Her mom's face had the kind of endeared expression she might wear while watching two toddlers bounce around in a playpen.

Ian's mom also got the chance to meet Nikkita's parents, telling them their daughter would be welcome to visit the Everson home anytime. "We love having company over," she said, patting her son on the shoulder, faltering before adding, "Especially these days."

Ian's face sobered, and Nikkita stopped to imagine what it must be like. To live in a home where the former man of the house, a husband and father, had passed away decades before anyone in his family would've thought he would.

Even so, Ian's mom wasn't merely making polite conversation that day. For the rest of Nikkita's high school sophomore year and through to a portion of her senior year, she made herself at home over at the Eversons' place plenty of times. Ian's mom and sister often had their own guests over, and sometimes everyone at the house congregated together. However, usually at some point while Nikkita was there, Ian would take her off to his dad's den.

"Ian Bean," she addressed him in a hushed voice the first time as she hung back from following him through the den's sliding wooden doors. There was something about the room's atmosphere, even obvious from the open doorway—an atmosphere distinct from the other parts of the house she'd been in.

Ian's gaze, as it made a pensive trip around the walls, held memory. Regret. Reverence. "We still call it Dad's, but it's actually mine now," he explained, walking over to a wall of the room's built-in shelves. "His books are in here." He moved toward an armoire on the other side of the room. "And it's the only place I have a TV all to myself."

Ian then turned to give Nikkita a reassuring look. "Come on in, Nikki. He would've liked you."

There couldn't be any hanging back from that. Nikkita took a respectful step into the room.

From then on, when Ian would take out and pop in DVDs of *Leave It to Beaver* to watch with Nikkita, it was always in the den, where the two of them would relax in side-by-side leather armchairs.

One Friday evening, soon after their first round with Season Three of the show had begun, Nikkita sat forward in her chair, staring at the screen of the television in the armoire and saying, "Hey. Ward's new den looks a lot like this one. Except with no computer and stuff, but yeah."

Ian's eyes slid toward Nikkita for a second, along with a half-smile. "You think so?"

Nikkita sat back, reevaluating this room and all of the books and wood and leather and fatherly essence residing here. "Was it on purpose?" she asked.

While Ian's smile didn't exactly leave, his gaze became more reflective, not moving away from the television this time. "I don't know," he mused, his voice low.

Because he left it at that, so did Nikkita. But it didn't matter that he didn't know. All at once, it seemed more than ever that *of course* this family television show, a black and white one from this century, was one that Ian would watch over and over again. Of course this den would be the room he'd watch it in.

For his own reasons, he now chose to watch the show with Nikkita.

When the two of them would work on homework together, it was often at Nikkita's house, where the environment was quieter for the most part, and Ian frequently invalidated the various claims he'd made by then about putting off his homework until breakfast on the days his assignments were due. Whenever he could, he would stay over longer after they'd finished studying, and Nikkita would share her music time with him in the rec room, where she loved to sit down at her keyboard.

"When'd you learn to play?" Ian asked once when Nikkita paused from her keyboard and grabbed up a remote control to change the CD in the stereo.

More music started, and Nikkita's eyes followed her fingers as she began playing chords on her instrument. "Mm. Didn't. Kinda taught myself. I'm no pro at it, but my brain can break music down better when I play along."

Ian stood listening, watching her for a minute. "You make up any of your own stuff?"

Nikkita shrugged, her fingers assisting her mind in playing around with a harmony. "Sort of. Nothing shareable yet."

"Oh. Someday?"

She looked up at him then, dreams rising in her eyes. "Most likely. Music's my first language. It's been speaking to me ever since my mom was still carrying me." She moved one hand away from the keys, spinning her fingers near her middle. "She says I would kick around the most in there whenever jazz or soul was playing."

Ian's head moved up and down, and he took a seat on the rec room couch. "So, music speaks to you, and you speak back."

Dreams in her eyes were met with accord. She didn't have to produce a smile then to feel one. "I sang a song for Renée. At my school's talent show." The disclosure, spoken barely a notch above the stereo's volume, was enough to bring a flicker of added interest, of empathy, to Ian's stare.

Nikkita's hands had stopped playing altogether. "Never really knew before then that I could stay on pitch while crying, if I had to." She looked downward, smiling now. "Had she been there, she would've threatened to sue me for damages if I went sharp or flat or croaky and embarrassed her in front of everybody." A chuckle escaped Nikkita's rasping throat.

She trailed a finger over the black and white keys before her, then brought her eyes back to Ian, her smile intended for him this time. "She would've gotten your jokes too, I think."

Ian did a double-take, even though he'd already been looking at Nikkita. "Yeah?" His eyebrows went up. "As bad as they are?"

A jazzy blast of horns from the stereo made Nikkita's skin tingle. Both her hands returned to the keyboard. "Even you can have a good day," she allowed, and Ian slapped a palm over his face, failing to conceal a laugh.

Where Nikkita's church life was concerned, her earning various solos in choir drew constructive critiques and pleased pats on the back from the youth choir director—as well as hearty compliments and high-fives from the youth pastor—but Nikkita's singing didn't place her in the social center of the youth ministry.

Still, now that she had a more personal social connection she didn't have at first, she was more motivated to participate in the group's activities outside of church, including trips to the roller skating rink. Aside from whatever he might or might not have been able to do on blades and ice, Ian wasn't bad at all on wheels. He and Nikkita would make their way around the rink together for some of the songs, with her hand in his.

For two high school baseball seasons, Nikkita went out to a good number of Ian's games. The sport hadn't held any particular interest for her for most of her life, but it was different now that she had someone to cheer for. Someone who would spot her up in the bleachers as easily as he could spot his mom and sister when they were there. Someone who got a kick out of Nikkita's cheers, which he claimed he could recognize even with everybody else's noise out there.

Nikkita once came close to making one of her cheers too recognizable. On her first occasion of seeing Ian hit a triple out on the field, she jumped to her feet and nearly cried out, "Ian Bean!"

While he, in his properly dirty uniform he hadn't yet changed out of, accompanied Nikkita on her walk through the parking lot after the game, she admitted the public slipup she'd almost made.

Ian told her he didn't mind. "We're good as long as you don't take it too far. I mean, if you started calling me 'Ian Evvv-ver-son hummm-ble bumblebee boo-boo' or anything like that in front of people, I'd have to get you for it."

"You'd have to get me?" Nikkita smirked up at him. "Well, what about in private? You'd be fine with something like 'humble bumblebee boo-boo' then?"

"Sure. Whatever. In *private*-private. So private that if extreme mush like that comes into your head, you keep it in your head and don't bother me with it."

As they arrived at the car Nikkita had borrowed from her dad, she turned to Ian with a challenge. "What if I sang it to you, though?"

Ian rested one hand on the car's roof and, dirty uniform and all, he leaned closer to Nikkita, smirking back with something that didn't quite have the edge that a smirk should. His warming voice dropped. "Playing with my emotions, Nik-Nik?"

Although her stomach did a pleasurable flip, Nikkita kept her tone casual as she reached up to tug down the bill of Ian's hat, the cleanest thing on him. "Hit the showers, slugger. Very good game, now enough *playing* for today. You've got homework to go do. No rushing and cramming it in at breakfast or you'll straight-up choke on your corn flakes one of these days."

"Hey!" Ian protested with a guffaw, his free hand going up to adjust his hat after her tampering. "'Slugger,' huh? So you speak baseball now?"

"Sure do, boo-boo." She eased Ian's other hand off of her dad's car.

During the middle of summer vacation preceding the start of Nikkita's junior year, she auditioned and earned the chance to sing in a variety talent showcase at a regional festival, held at an amphitheater a county away from her town. Along with Nikkita's parents, the Eversons were among those in her cheering section, which also included some of her schoolmates and a few members of youth group, Jayme possibly being the loudest cheerer of that specific bunch.

When Nikkita went to find her section of people after the show, her parents were first in fussing over her, presenting her with a bright assortment of flowers and balloons they'd snuck off to pick up at some point before the show started.

"Hope the balloons aren't too much," Nikkita's mom told her, "but this is a big deal, baby! We're so proud of you. You were excellent!"

"Thanks so much," Nikkita enthused, waving off her mom's uncertainty about the balloons while her dad, maneuvering around balloon strings, bent to plant a kiss on Nikkita's forehead.

The Eversons then approached her with more flowers, Ian's mom informing her that "he picked the color" as Ian handed Nikkita a bouquet.

Roses. Ones she might have assumed to be red on first glance, but they were actually a vibrant orange.

"They're gorgeous," Nikkita added to her word of thanks to the family, cradling their offering in her full arms.

"Appropriate, then," Ian replied at a level evidently meant only for Nikkita's ears. She looked up at him, somewhat amazed to find him blushing. Was it because he'd dared to make such a comment while other people were around? Not caring if that was the case, Nikkita gave him a smile meant only for his eyes, regardless of the fact that most of her cheering section would see it.

That autumn, Ian was rather secretive concerning the details of a certain Saturday afternoon outing he picked Nikkita up for. Once they came to a stoplight past the half-hour mark of their commute, Ian reached down behind the passenger seat of his car.

"Feel free to put this on. We're getting close," he told Nikkita, and she gave a little gasp as he produced his letterman jacket from behind the seat. He wore the jacket on pep rally days at his school, but she herself had only seen it once before, when he'd obliged her urgent request for him to bring it to the den and wear it for her while they watched an especially sporty *Beaver* episode.

Ian kept the rest of his secret for the short remainder of their drive, and Nikkita soon had trouble controlling the grin that kept popping out every other second as she and Ian took two available stools at the counter inside of an old-fashioned ice cream parlor.

A parlor complete with a soda fountain.

"See?" Ian held out proud hands toward the establishment in general, a place brought to life by a moderate crowd of dessert eaters along with oldies tunes bopping and crooning through the air. "Told you they're from this century."

Nikkita laughed, her frame relatively engulfed by Ian's large garment of varsity glory pulled over her shoulders. "And it took you how long to find one to prove they still exist?"

Ian, using one foot to swivel himself back and forth on his stool with satisfied triumph, didn't deign to answer that.

When a server came and asked what the two of them would have, and Ian repeated the question to Nikkita, she tipped her head to the side, her eyebrow arching at Ian. "A no-brainer, but thank you for asking."

After a jolly snicker, he duly ordered two black and whites, both with whipped cream.

As it turned out, however, their no-brainer order required a bit more brain afterward, since the fizzy vanilla and chocolate contents of their tall soda glasses did an unasked-for job of whetting their appetites. Given their mutual disinclination to spend a longish return commute talking over growling stomachs, Ian and Nikkita ordered grilled cheese sandwiches and bowls of tomato soup, which were two of only a few non-dessert items on the menu.

"Soup, sandwiches, and sodas," Ian said with a pat to his stomach, dipping a corner of one diagonal half of his sandwich into his soup. "Not over-ordering at all."

It took a minute for Nikkita to shuffle back into her memory and catch on, at which point a chortle burst from her. "Nope. Guess not. Just ordering out of order. Charity, faith, and..." She held up half of her own sandwich. "And hope not to go home hungry."

"Mm-*mumph*-mmp," Ian answered with a bob of his head in between swallows of cheesy bread and tomato. He finished his bite and smacked his lips. "Not really out of order, though. Because there's faith, hope, and charity, and the greatest of these is..."

With wide eyes and a jubilant smile, Nikkita pointed toward the busy fountain behind the counter. "Is soda!" she finished for Ian, and he had to get his next bite down in between a series of chuckles.

As Nikkita did some of her own head-bobbing, hers to the beat of the oldies hit now sparkling its way through the place, she had a sudden impression of nostalgia. She thought of letterman sweaters instead of jackets, old music that hadn't always been old, and soda fountains at drugstores on any number of street corners rather than rare fountains at special places you had to really search for and make special drives to reach.

Looking around the ice cream parlor, she imagined a sunny and starry simplicity to young people's social lives, wondering if it was the kind of idea the adults at church had in mind when they admonished the youth to live clean, holy lifestyles.

No cussing. No music or movies you wouldn't listen to or watch with a granny and a reverend in the room. No engaging in vulgar conversations. No wild partying. No staying out past midnight.

No sex.

If there was anything Pastor Tyler emphasized in his sermons as much as young people's legitimate need for healing, it was their calling to sexual purity.

"You all haven't reached the point where you can seek out the security of marriage," Pastor Tyler had told his crowd of teenage listeners at a recent Wednesday night service, "so you have to watch out for danger around you. To watch out for those convincing voices telling you to go for it. The voices of peer pressure. Voices in the media. Voices in your head." He crossed his eyes, flapping a "talking" hand beside one of his ears, earning a mild hum of laughter from his audience before he went on.

"A lot of teens think they're grown enough to handle sex, but they're not. Sex is more complex than your flesh and hormones may be telling you it is, and I'm sure you know at least something about where promiscuity can lead. Unwanted pregnancies. Diseases. Complicated and broken relationships that result in broken hearts.

"Not all pain in life is escapable, but God doesn't want you running around getting broken even more by getting into situations you could totally avoid. He wants so much for you to be healed and whole and not to mess up the few teen years you've got. He wants you to trust the process of growing up, instead of dabbling or jumping into things you aren't ready for yet. So trust the process. Patience pays off, I promise.

"And to all of you beautiful young ladies," Pastor Tyler said with a smile and a shift in his stance. "You have to understand that it can be especially challenging for guys who want to stay pure. God made guys to be pursuers, so they're easily turned on by what they see. More easily than you are, ladies. That's because men are made to pursue sex with their wives, but obviously, guys your age don't have wives yet.

"So help out your brothers in Christ, sisters. Show love to our guys by not dressing or acting like the sex objects the world wants women to be. Your brothers need modesty from you so they can stay focused on the things of God, amen?"

That wasn't the only time at church that Nikkita heard anything in relation to young ladies and focusing on God, or hindering others from that focus. At a youth choir practice one Saturday, Minister Kate dismissed the guy members some minutes early so that she could have a private word with the girls.

"All right, sweeties." Minister Kate folded her hands in front of her. "I was at a church leadership meeting this past week, and a concern from the church's suggestion box was brought to my attention. Certain members of the congregation have found some of you to be a distraction when our choir sings at morning services. You all have been good about watching the length of your dresses and skirts on Sundays, but be sure you're wearing the proper undergarments for support. If you haven't already, you should start wearing sports bras to church."

As that pointer had brought heat to Nikkita's face, she'd refused to squirm or to take a peek down at herself.

"You know how much I encourage praising God with open joy," Minister Kate continued, "so no need to feel like you have to start standing there like singing statues. That's not what we're about. But while I'm up here directing, with my backside to the congregation, do you ever see me, oh, shaking my hips? No. Because corporate worship means being considerate of others in the room. I wouldn't want the 'move of me' to distract anyone's focus from the move of God.

"So when you sway or you bounce your knees and clap to the music, bring your hands up and hold your arms in close to your chest. Don't go overboard like you're trying to *squeeze* yourself stiff, but just hold yourself together." She gave a brief demonstration and a shaky giggle. "See? This works fine. Bouncing knees are good. But letting your chi-chis do the cha-cha in church? That's another story. Keep those babies as still as possible."

A few responding giggles echoed through the group of teen girls, but as some of them stood there with looks of distaste, embarrassment, or worry on their faces, Minister Kate sighed and said, "Look, you guys. Ladies. It's okay. It's a thought adjustment you have to make, that's all. But to be honest, singing in choir shouldn't be the only times you're thinking about this stuff. You're not little girls anymore. You're young women, and you have to be mindful of that."

Minister Kate spread her hands toward the girls. "For instance, I know some of you are naturally touchy-feely, and that's totally fine. But at this stage in your life, you really shouldn't be hugging guys as much as some of you do. I know it might be sweet and innocent to you, but trust me, it doesn't feel just sweet and innocent to the guy you're standing chest to chest with. Not even if the guy loves Jesus." She wrapped her arms around herself. "If you're a hugger and that's how you genuinely show love, hug guys from the side, not the front. Give them a quick squeeze and let that be that. They'll still get your message of love without it feeling like a full-frontal kind of thing. Does that make sense?"

Nikkita's cheeks had still been burning when she left that choir rehearsal.

She never felt great after sermons or talks like that in church, but was it due to adolescent pride on her part? Was it resistance to adults—ones who weren't related to her—telling her what to do, even when it came to personal matters like hugs and underwear?

"Well. It's different when you're in a choir," Nikkita had told herself later on, after Minister Kate's talk about chi-chis doing the cha-cha. All kinds of people who presented or performed in front of audiences had to adhere to wardrobe requirements befitting whatever stages they were on. The youth choir director wasn't trying to be dictatorial.

Nikkita had stood examining her curves in the full-length mirror in her bedroom that day. The effect of sports bras would mess with the look of her outfits, doing a poorer job of evening out her pear shape than her push-up bras did. Besides, discounting some of her earliest, ultra imaginative attempts at putting together her own ensembles as a small child, neither of her parents had ever given her a tip or the notion that she was an inappropriate dresser.

With that in mind, along with the fact that Nikkita didn't do the shakiest or bounciest moving to the music in church anyway, she decided she'd go on wearing the bras that were the best styles for her outfits.

Was that rebellious of her? When she didn't feel right about those certain sermons she sat through, was it due to what the Bible and the church leadership would call her "flesh," the sinful nature?

Pastor Paul would go to those sticky places in some Sunday services, preaching against carnality, adultery, fornication, and lustful temptation. In contrast, he'd preach in favor of self-control and modest women while declaring the blessing and satisfaction of holy matrimony, mixing his declarations with words of praise for his wife. Still, Nikkita wondered more about sensuality preaching from a youth pastor who also upheld matrimony as the romantic standard and the way to sexual security while he himself wasn't married.

"He's a man of God," Nikkita would reason in initial answer to her wonderings. Telling the church's young people what they needed to hear was Pastor Tyler's duty. But without having a wife to fulfill the roles that he and Pastor Paul said that wives would indeed fulfill for their husbands, did Pastor Tyler live his life feeling unsafe from the prevalent danger of sex, the danger he often warned the youth group about?

If Nikkita should feel in danger anywhere, she figured her friendship with Ian would be the place. He was a warm-blooded guy, the two of them did hug sometimes, and since the day he'd shown up at Greyridge for her, she'd been growing closer to him than to any other male she wasn't related to.

Yet, ever since Greyridge, Nikkita had never felt anything less than safe with Ian.

That was a feeling worth trusting. Wasn't it?

"Nik-Nik? You okay?"

Nikkita gave her head a shake, blinking hard. "Hm?" With one hand, she adjusted Ian's letterman jacket on her shoulders, unsure of how many minutes might have gone by while she sat here spacing out in the ice cream parlor. "Sorry. Just thinking."

"'Bout what?" Ian waved a hand in front of her eyes. "Your face got intense."

Nikkita pushed her brooding aside and smiled at her lunch companion. "It was super sweet of you to find this place and bring me here, Bean."

Something bashful crept into Ian's look before he shrugged it away. "Nah. This is just one big 'I told you so.'" He pointed at his letterman jacket. "Pop my collar for me, would ya'?"

"Gladly." Nikkita put down the portion of sandwich she'd been holding and reached for Ian, zeroing in on the collar of his shirt.

"Whoa—Nikkita!" Ian and his shirt dodged her grabby fingers just in time, and she barely held in a mischievous snort.

No, she didn't feel anything less than safe in Ian Everson's presence.

On a different note, there turned out to be some occasions when Nikkita spent time in Ian's presence, technically, without knowing it. She wasn't alerted to it until after the close of one of the many pre-service prayer times she spent in the church's chapel.

She was usually one of the first to arrive in the chapel room, taking her spot near a wall where she'd have her preferred view out of the front windows. On Wednesdays especially, she'd remain still for an extra minute after prayer to prepare herself for the switch from the chapel's peaceful atmosphere to the youth's loud and electric celebrating in the sanctuary. So, she wouldn't see who all else had come to the chapel, and it was by chance one Wednesday when she rose from her seat after prayer and turned toward the chapel doors in time to get a glimpse of Ian disappearing through them.

"I wasn't going to bring this up," she spoke up a few days later from her place at her keyboard, letting the music on the rec room stereo go on while she paused from playing along. "Since you haven't said anything."

Ian didn't open his eyes or stir from his position on the couch. He was slouched down with his ankles crossed, his arms folded, and his head resting on a back cushion. "What about?"

Nikkita waited to see if he'd look at her, but when he didn't, she took up her remote, lowering the volume on the stereo. "Do you go to pre-service prayer all the time? Or were you only there this past Wednesday?"

Ian's eyes glided open to stare up at the rec room ceiling. "I've started going sometimes, when I can make it." One of his shoulders budged in a shrug. "Never really thought about going until you told me you do. I assumed it was only for the adults, or whatever. But lately I've been feeling like I should be doing more to get ready."

Nikkita's thoughts turned over his last phrase. "Get ready?"

His arms slid out of their folded position, his gaze still toward the ceiling. "I mean, I do my best to keep my grades up. And I play baseball. I take summer jobs. I'm in choir at church. But now that me and my mom have started looking into colleges and prep courses for entrance exams, I feel like I should have a better idea of what I'm gonna do. With my life."

Ian sat up, finally looking at Nikkita, his next words almost getting lost in the music even though she'd lowered the volume. "I'm not ready," he stressed.

Because his voice might have shaken on those words, Nikkita decided against turning the stereo further down or off. Sometimes music made it safer to say things.

"Oh," she said, carefully setting aside the remote. "Well. You have time. We both do." She took a chance at a smile, which she hoped looked reassuring. "We're seventeen. Not exactly grownups yet."

Ian shook his head. "I know, I know. But it's different with you. You have music." His hands indicated her keyboard, the stereo, the room. The world. "That's what you're gonna do. It's in your soul, in your bones. In your amazing voice. You were born for it."

The affirmation came from him so plainly, as if no one would ever think twice about it.

Even as good as his declaration made Nikkita feel, it didn't stop her from letting practicality weigh in. "Not every talented singer out there makes a whole life out of it."

Ian's hand moved, nudging her comment to one side of an invisible table. Maybe nudging it over the edge. "You will, though. At some point, if you want to, you will. It's like I can see it."

His eyes veered off into space before him. "But when I look at me, just me, five or ten years out from now, I hardly see anything." He passed a hand in front of him, waving through fog or smoke or a semblance of nothingness. "I mean, for around here, I'm pretty good at baseball, but not enough for a career doing that. I need God to give me a clearer picture of what to do."

Nikkita stared at him, staring into space.

When you look at you—just you?

But five or ten years out from now, it won't be just you.

You'll figure it out. That's what college years are for.

You're an incredible guy, Ian. You'll do something incredible...

Nikkita's consciousness teemed with so much she could tell him. Yet, when he looked at her again, the weight of something she couldn't define reached out and pressed her through his gaze. None of the words she could think of seemed the right match for that weight.

Both of Ian's hands had fallen to his sides on the couch, sitting there empty. "I was supposed to be talking about all this with my dad," he said.

Oh. There it was. *Of course.* Nikkita's insides dropped.

Ian continued. "Before I started driving, he used to tell me to get the kiddie stuff out of my system while I could, 'cause the nitty-gritty talks about my future would start once I got my license." He deepened his voice, holding up an authoritative finger. "'This world has enough aimless men as it is, Ian. If you'll be ready for the responsibility of driving yourself around, you'll be ready for direction.'"

One corner of Ian's lips hiked upward as he lowered his finger. "I thought it was corny because he would sound all 'manly man' about it, but really, I was looking forward to our man-to-man phase as much as he was." His partial smile faded. "My uncle Donnie is all right to talk to whenever I see him. He's making good out of his life. Your dad is cool too. And I guess Pastor Tyler would probably give good advice if I ever asked him. He says his office door is always open."

Ian gave his head another shake and slouched back onto the couch. "They're not my dad, though," he pointed out, his voice breaking as it rose a notch. "They're not like him." He let his head fall back to its previous spot, his voice also falling. Again. "I just want to talk to him. That's all." His hand came up to cover his eyes. "I want to talk to my dad. You know?"

Nikkita's insides hadn't lifted. Yes, she did know. She also knew enough to recognize that she didn't know.

She wasn't a son. Wasn't a son who'd lost his father. Wasn't a fill-in for what that son had lost.

Still, with all that she was, she moved away from her keyboard and went to the couch, lowering herself beside Ian, leaning back into the cushion behind her. In the company of manifest grief, she simply sat there.

But she didn't simply sit. Through the atmosphere of the room, the music played on: all that was within, beneath, and around it. Even more beyond it, like the verses and refrain of a sacred hymn riding the air, still profound even when the literal lyrics went unsung.

There Nikkita sat waiting. Seeking. Hoping. Requesting.
My God? Please.
Sensing.
My God.
Knowing.

At first, she wasn't aware when Ian shifted, but as soon as his face settled down on her shoulder, she angled her own face closer in, catching the crisp scent of his hair. She brought a hand up to his cheek, her fingertips skimming warm vanilla. The pad of her thumb took a tender lead, smoothing over tears that had slipped down from his closed eyes to dampen the skin bearing a precious spread of bean speckles.

Nikkita didn't feel anything less than safe in Ian Everson's presence. Down to her core, she in turn wanted to be a safe place for him. Though she couldn't be everything he needed in life, she wanted to be this.

Here for him. Safe.

Chapter Six

OVER A GOOD PORTION of her time in the youth ministry, it didn't strike Nikkita as strange that after Ian, the guy at church she received the most attention from was Pastor Tyler. It stood to reason that a shepherd in charge of a teenage flock would take notice of the individual sheep under his watch, as much as he was able.

Pastor Tyler wouldn't neglect to comment on the blessing of Nikkita's singing after this or that service. He'd remind her of her great worth to God. He'd tell her that his office door was open if she ever needed to come see him. He'd come to her relatively private spot around the corner of the sound booth's wall in the sanctuary during prayer times at Saturday choir practices. He'd crouch down near her place on the floor, asking if she wanted prayer for anything.

Most times, knowing that the youth pastor would only take a minute before he'd move on to other choir members, Nikkita would pull only a part of her attention through the soft music playing in the room, and she'd make no specific requests.

One Saturday, however, she told Pastor Tyler she wanted prayer about her schoolwork.

"Physics class, actually," she said. "It's too late to drop the class for an 'incomplete,' but somehow my brain isn't clicking with the assignments at all. I don't want my GPA to be slipping while I'm starting to apply to colleges."

"Ah. Well, that's easy." Pastor Tyler nodded, then shook his head. "I mean, not easy, but there's a solution for students who know the all-knowing God. The Bible says the Holy Spirit will lead us into all truth and teach us all things. Not just spiritual truth or spiritual things but *all* things. So when you go to class or you sit down to do your homework, first acknowledge the Holy Spirit as your teacher. Ask Him to help you understand physics better, and He will."

Nikkita's eyes grew round. "Huh. Wow. Never thought of that." She chewed on that idea for a second before she raised her hands, pretending to give a giddy clap. "Goodie! That does sound easy. Better than a cheat sheet."

"Uh, yeah, no." Pastor Tyler kept his voice down as he laughed. "Better than cheating, yes, but He won't just spoon-feed you all the answers. God gave us brains to study with. So be thankful for His leading and trust the process of learning. Trust your heavenly teacher while you study, and see what happens. All right?" He opened his hands. "Let's pray about it."

Pleased with the sound of his advice, Nikkita gave him a nod. "Okay."

With nothing to lose, she took Pastor Tyler's words to heart in the following days, approaching her physics studies with a more prayerful, thankful mindset. Soon, deciding it would be better not to limit that mindset to physics, she began approaching all of her schoolwork with a different attitude.

A couple of Saturdays later, Pastor Tyler again came around the sound booth's wall during the youth choir's prayer time. He hadn't even crouched down before Nikkita looked up from her place on the floor to deliver an excited murmur just above the music playing over her head.

"An eighty-four! I got an eighty-four on my physics test yesterday," she told Pastor Tyler, allowing a conceding chortle. "The homework still isn't fun, but you were right. I've been asking Him to teach me, and He's helping me understand the work."

A grin to match her excitement spread over Pastor Tyler's face. "Yes! Way to go, Nikkita." He did crouch then but did so closer to her than his usual spot, lifting his hand. "And it wasn't me. It's the Bible that's right."

Nikkita smiled her agreement, lifting her hand as well for a high-five, and Pastor Tyler gave her one. His palm then lingered against hers, his fingers shifting to link loosely with hers as he said, "He cares for you so much. Even in the everyday things."

It took an extra second or two for that last comment to register with Nikkita. Her train of thought had come to a brief stutter, and Pastor Tyler's fingers slid from hers, ending his light clasp.

As was his habit, he didn't take up much more of her time. After he moved on, Nikkita sat listening to the music in the sanctuary, intending to continue praying on her own.

There with her intentions, she had trouble concentrating.

"He cares for you so much."

"Nikki? You okay?" Ian asked as he walked Nikkita out to her mom's car after choir practice that day.

She shook herself a bit, sent a vague smile in Ian's direction, and didn't answer him. A frown came over his face, but he didn't press the issue.

How many times had Pastor Tyler given Nikkita reminders about God's care, concern, and approval since she'd started coming to church?

"Don't be silly," she took to telling herself aloud now and then when she'd think about it. Could she say how many countless times celebratory high-fives morphed into happy hand clasps and handshakes in people's everyday lives, and no one meant or read anything more into those gestures? Countless times for sure, she figured.

Nonetheless, somewhere along the line during her junior year, Nikkita found herself starting to look around while she was at church and at youth group activities, watching Pastor Tyler. Watching his interactions with the women at church, especially teen girls. What she saw in those interactions were smiles, laughter, handshakes, and high-fives.

She felt pretty ridiculous. Ridiculous and a little guilty for watching. Guilty for even wondering about it in the first place, for having difficulty shaking off feelings that didn't seem right, including when it came to sensuality sermons. A person shouldn't allow their sinful nature to pervert their view of what was good or otherwise harmless.

"He's a man of God," Nikkita would reiterate to herself. A man of God in the house of God where she'd first experienced the wonder of prayer and couldn't get enough of it since. The place where she'd joined a choir that taught her more about music, corporate worship, and making good presentations onstage. The place where she received biblical teaching every week and learned more about the Spirit. The place where she could be a part of wholesome activities with young people of faith.

Moreover, it was more than likely that she never would have met Ian without this place.

"So. Don't be silly about this," she'd tell herself, and try to move her thoughts elsewhere.

Nikkita knew it wasn't impossible for her not to feel weird about something at church when she didn't have to. She'd imagined that she might start feeling too different about pre-service prayer once she found out that Ian came there sometimes. Would it somehow seem less special to her, now that she knew she wasn't the only teenager who joined adults in the chapel? Would the knowledge of Ian's being in the room wind up distracting her?

After tussling with a measure of worry over it, she'd continued her routine of getting to the chapel early and also delaying at the end after other people started to leave. Once she found that she had no added trouble waiting, listening, seeking, hoping, requesting, finding, resting, and sometimes quietly crying in that cherished atmosphere, she wondered why she'd bothered with worry over it at all.

Nikkita also cried every once in a while during prayer times at choir practice. On a Saturday afternoon during her senior year, when Pastor Tyler came around the corner of the sound booth wall in the sanctuary, it was much like the first time he'd ever found Nikkita over there. She had to dry her eyes with her sweatshirt sleeve when she looked up at him.

"Oh. Did I startle you, Nikkita?"

She shook her head, sniffling, still full of the inexplicable encounter she'd been having, but she did her best to pull her attention forward through the room's soft music.

Pastor Tyler came and sat on the floor beside her, resting back against the sound booth wall. Nikkita scooted over slightly to give him room, keeping her bent knees together and angled down to the side, as though she were wearing a skirt instead of jeans.

Pastor Tyler sighed, keeping his voice low. "Not everyone knows what it's like to be in the presence this way, when you can't help it and everything just"—he drew a hand over his face, trailing his fingers down from his eyes—"comes out."

Nikkita's eyes filled again. She blinked to keep control.

After taking a second to study her, possibly waiting to see if she would shed more tears, Pastor Tyler murmured, "You've known me for some time now. Has it been two years?" He didn't pause for an answer. "I'm not sure why you've never come to see me in my office, but again, if there's anything you ever want to talk to me about—if you need to let some stuff come out, and you think no one will understand..." His mouth slanted with something like regret. "It may be that even your parents wouldn't understand."

His mention of Nikkita's parents caught her unawares. It stung.

She still remembered the slow reactions her mom and dad had back when she was a sophomore, on the evening she'd told them she was joining a youth choir at church. The odd looks they used to give her when they saw her reading her Bible at home had eventually turned into looks of careful indifference. Her parents had come to some Sunday services and the church's Holy Week and Christmas programs to hear Nikkita sing, but they still had made no regular habit of coming to church with her.

Why did it seem she was yet unable to explain to them what had been happening to her since the first time she'd gone and sat in the church's chapel room? Wouldn't it all sound corny or crazy if she tried to articulate it, earning her another phase of her parents' odd looks? Or would her parents possibly answer with scornful remarks?

Nikkita dabbed under her eyes with the cuff of her sweatshirt sleeve.

"Sometimes," Pastor Tyler went on, "you need to talk to someone who's seen more of life than you but who isn't there to get on your case about anything. Someone who wants to listen to you." His head inclined a degree to one side. "To hear that voice of yours," he said, bringing one hand up to his chest. "To hear the desires of your heart."

With that comment, and the sight of Pastor Tyler's hand on his chest, Nikkita's immediate thoughts came to a virtual standstill.

Pastor Tyler's head went from side to side. "I've found that most young people are jumbled bundles of energy and hormones. They don't need much more than typical pointers, prayer, and time to grow up and figure things out." He gave a self-deprecating smile, raising a confessing hand. "I was a jumbled-up boy myself, once upon a time." He chuckled, shook his head again, and sobered, his hand coming down. "But lately, I've been wrestling a lot over something, and I've finally had to face it."

It wasn't the way his eyes kept a hold on Nikkita's that made her tears stop up. That had already happened when her thoughts came to a stop.

"I've had to face that I'm called to discern when such a special person..." Pastor Tyler's gaze softened, and he inched closer to Nikkita on the floor. "A person with such a gift and maturity about her—she may actually need a safe place to bring her heart and explore her desires."

Nikkita's spine went painfully stiff.

"What did I tell you? Such a pearl. What a gift. Genuine and mature."

Her back, partially settled against the sound booth wall, began prickling with perspiration, as did her chest.

"Nikkita is on the ball. That kind of maturity is wonderful to see."

All at once, the heat gathering underneath her sweatshirt was becoming unbearable.

Pastor Tyler's look resembled resignation. Surrender. "Sometimes the process of building unique relationships is beyond our understanding. But the Bible says we aren't supposed to lean on our own understanding anyway." One of his hands moved, and Nikkita was mistaken in the split-second that she assumed he'd be reaching for his chest again. "We have to trust the process," he said.

That hand of his moved forward, hovering low, coming to make a smooth landing on Nikkita's thigh.

Nearly everything within her froze in an instant before her blood took up the baleful beating of drums in her ears. Prayer music was still playing in the room, but her hearing couldn't find it.

"My door is open to you, as always," Pastor Tyler yielded on a sonorous note, the brush of his fingers on her thigh seeming to burn through the denim covering her skin. "If you ever need me."

One of her tense hands trembled, her fingers twitching as they came close to curling. To clenching. But they didn't make it there. In a moment of indecision, instinct lost its grip as reiteration stole over it.

"He's a man of God."

Pastor Tyler didn't ask her if she had any prayer requests before he eased away from her, rose to his feet, and disappeared around the corner of the sound booth.

Nikkita remained where she was, shaking. Sweating her soul out. Beginning to breathe hard. Suddenly struggling to catch any breath at all.

In the haze of the last few minutes, she'd asked no questions. She'd voiced no protests. She'd failed to find any shred of her voice whatsoever. Instead, she'd sat at the mercy of limbs that had also failed by locking up on her, her senses making little sense of whatever it was that had just happened here.

Whatever it was that incited this horrendous beating in her ears. Beating that left only a part of her hearing available to pick up the inevitable hum of choir members greeting each other, laughing here and there, preparing to head for their places on the sanctuary platform.

After tearful prayer times at church, Nikkita usually snatched up her purse beside her and took out her compact to check on her mascara. She snatched up her purse now but didn't open it as she got on her free hand and both knees, clumsy and shuddery as she crawled on the floor around the back way of the sound booth, poking her head around the back corner, checking to make sure that only Minister Kate and the choir members were the ones still in the room. Then, Nikkita pushed to her feet, made a beeline for the sanctuary doors, escaped into the foyer, and shot straight through it and out of the church building, running through the parking lot for her mom's car.

Later that day, Ian messaged her by text on her cellphone, asking why she'd disappeared before the choir's singing had gotten started. Nikkita, currently shut away in her bedroom and curled up in a ball on her bed, fidgeted with her phone for a minute, debating about text messaging back.

In the end, she didn't do it. She sat up and searched through the handful of numbers stored in her phone, venturing to make a call instead.

The phone barely rang twice on the other end before her call was picked up.

"Wow! Nikkita!" Jayme's voice sprang into her ear. "You're calling me? You never call me. You never call hardly anybody, do you? Aww. I feel so special!"

Nikkita scooted over on her bed so that she could lean against her pillows and headboard for support. "Hi, Jayme. Are you alone right now?"

"Not quite. Why? *Ooo*—say no more. Girl talk? Awesome! Hold on a sec." There was a pause and some shuffling on Jayme's end, along with what sounded like the slamming of a door, and she sprang back on. "'Kay, I'm alone now. So what's up? You wanna talk about Ian?"

Nikkita's forehead furrowed. "Ian? Why?"

"*Why*? Ooh, maybe because it's so obvious you two will be the first ones from youth group to get married. He's probably going to ask you before we're all even out of college."

Had this been any other time, Nikkita would have been taken aback by that and would've stopped to sort through it with Jayme. On the other hand, had this been any other time, Nikkita wouldn't be talking to Jayme on the phone.

Setting Ian completely aside, Nikkita told Jayme, "I have a question about Pastor Tyler."

"Yeah? Oh! Okay. Shoot."

After taking a deep breath, Nikkita dove in. "Does he ever ask to see you in his office?"

A giggle accompanied Jayme's carefree reply. "Sure. His office is open to everybody."

Nikkita's eyes half-rolled in frustration. "I know. But is it ever almost like he's... Is it like he's singling you out?"

"Um, why?" Freedom from care was quick to desert Jayme's voice. "What've you heard?" Her tone had dropped, low and hard. "Junk from Sandra?"

Surprise and bewilderment tugged Nikkita's mouth open, but she produced no answer.

Jayme sucked her teeth, and her hushed voice sounded all the closer, as though she'd stepped into a box. Or into a closet. "She's been getting on my case lately, thinking I see too much of Tyler. She threatened to tell my parents if I don't tell them myself." The huff of a sigh parted her words. "As if somebody like Sandra could ever understand. She's so…high school, sometimes." Jayme's bitter crack of laughter was more like a grunt. "Well, I don't know how much more junk or gossip might start flying around since she's apparently running her mouth now. So I want you to hear this from *me*."

Before the coming explanation even started, Nikkita's stomach was already sinking.

"Yes, I see Tyler kind of a lot," Jayme admitted, "because he gets me. People think I'm just bubbly ol' Jayme, like nothing ever stresses me out or anything. Well, *newsflash*, it's hard being 'up' all the time. I can be down or be whatever I feel when it's me and Tyler, and he doesn't judge me." The bitterness drained from her voice. "It heals me to be with him."

Nikkita willed the beating in her ears not to start back up. She needed to hear. "I-I'm sorry to ask this," she fumbled, "but to be with him…how?"

"How?" Jayme sounded as if the question were a needless one. "Natural. That's how." She gave another sigh. "A lot of people are too legalistic or narrow-minded to get it, but God gives us natural ways to connect with people in unique relationships. To experience wholeness together." Her voice fell to a whisper. "For intimate healing."

The prickling of sweat on Nikkita's body this time was very much like stinging.

Jayme wasn't finished. "And, um, not to overshare, but in case you're thinking it, because a lot of super-churchy adults try to tell us that *everything* intimate is bad—it isn't fornication unless you're doing what can get you pregnant." Her statement had a telling note of confidence in it. "Like, the actual baby-making way is meant only for husbands and wives, but most teenagers are too immature not to try it that way if they're alone together and start exploring. So adults go overboard and tell them, 'Don't do *anything* with *anybody*. Ever. Nothing more than holding hands till your wedding night. Or else.'" There was something brittle about Jayme's snicker. "It takes maturity for two consenting Christians to keep the right boundaries while they're being intimate. The process is spiritual, really."

Nikkita's free hand went up to hold her head, which had started to throb. "Is that...is that what he tells you? All that?"

"Tyler? What he tells me the most is that I'm a pearl of great price and that I deserve to be cared for. He sees me and gets me. He has for years."

The tips of Nikkita's fingers dug into her hair, boring into her scalp, aching. Her vocal cords barely mustered the strength to say, "We... You're only in high school, still."

A severe moment of dead silence reached Nikkita's ear before Jayme spoke back up, slowly. "Oh, no. Don't you go getting all 'high school' on me too, Nikkita. A man with discernment can recognize when a young woman is grown-up for her age, and it isn't like Tyler has ever forced me into anything. He already saw that I was different from other girls when I was twelve, but he waited. I mean, back in Bible times, I could've been engaged by that age. But no, Tyler waited for me till I turned fourteen and he could be extra sure I was ready for him. He was patient, and patience pays off."

Memory, incredulity, and horror made Nikkita's stomach churn.

"He's always...gentle with me too," Jayme continued. "No hitting or crazy stuff when we—when I go to see him. So don't go thinking of him as a child abuser or anything like that. I mean, I'm not a child anyway."

"But, Jayme, if you...if you were only fourteen when he started... Not even—"

"What? It wasn't even legal? Well, Christianity itself isn't even legal everywhere. Some things are bigger than the laws of this world." Jayme's voice began to thicken. "Tyler is just so awesome, and it'll suck if I have to lose him because of stupid rumors and judgy people who try to force everything into a box." She gave another grunt. "They even try to force God into a box, 'cause they lean too much on their own understanding instead of the Spirit."

Nikkita couldn't stop the throbbing. The churning. She fought for an effective reply. Something that would turn this conversation around—something to let her know that everything she thought she'd heard over the last stretch of minutes was nothing more than a misunderstanding.

Yet, all Nikkita managed to do was to repeat herself. In disbelief. In desperation. "Is that what he tells you?" she whispered.

"God? Tyler?" Jayme seemed ready to answer the question at hand before she didn't, her tone shifting. "Now, look. I told you all this because I know you're really into prayer and worship. I figured you're spiritually minded, not like those stuffy airheads that thump the Bible all day without even knowing what it actually stands for. So I was hoping you would get it. It doesn't sound like you do, though."

Nikkita's eyes slid to a heavy, searing close. No, but she did get it. She couldn't take how much she got it.

She got it almost as much as she didn't get it at all.

Jayme was then rather swift in saying she needed to go, and she got off the phone.

Nikkita curled back into a ball on her bed.

Though she hadn't planned it at the time, the day she ran out of choir practice early turned out to be her last day at that church. A couple of days later, she sent a single email, one to the youth choir director, saying she could no longer be in choir as she focused on school, and she thanked the director for all of her support and instruction.

Nikkita's parents made no comment on the first Sunday morning when she slept in and stayed home. On the following Wednesday evening, when she didn't hurry through her spaghetti and meatballs at the dinner table, her mom asked her, "Um, won't you be late for church if you don't get a move on?"

Nikkita looked from her mom to her dad, trying to laugh. "Oh, no biggie. It's getting kind of boring there. Same old, same old, every week. I wasn't learning anything new in choir anymore either, so I dropped it. Minister Kate's cool with it, since I want to focus on school anyway." She speared a meatball with her fork. "My teachers say that while college acceptance letters are coming in, we have to watch out for the senioritis bug. So I really need to keep my brain on school now. And probably not hang out as much while I work on my own music."

Nikkita's mom gave a faint nod. "Oh. I see." A look then passed between the Creighton couple, but if either of them had anything more to say on the church issue, they didn't say it to their daughter that evening.

The phone call with Jayme turned out not to be the only call Nikkita endured around that point. After a little over half a month of her absence from church and her failure to answer most of her text messages, Ian finally dared to call her instead.

Nikkita was careful in her explanation to him. "My dad said from the start that my participation in choir would be a plus for college applications. He was right, and I've been accepted into the school I want. I've told you about their music program."

"Oh, yeah. Yeah. I didn't forget that," Ian confirmed, though something in his tone sounded unsure.

"Yeah." Nikkita tried to keep her attitude relaxed. "So I don't have to stay in choir now."

"What do you mean? You haven't been coming to church only to be in choir. Quitting choir doesn't mean you have to quit coming to everything." When Nikkita didn't reply to that, Ian's voice dipped to a doleful mutter. "It even feels like you've quit me, past couple weeks."

Pain and guilt shot through Nikkita. *Wait. Breathe. Keep it together.* She cleared her throat. "Oh, don't say that. We've been church buddies, Be—Ian," she told him, deciding to keep her unavoidable declaration simple. Straightforward. "But I won't be at church anymore."

"We aren't just church buddies. You know that." Ian's answer was a quick one before he paused, possibly replaying Nikkita's declaration to himself. "But why won't you be there?" he asked, receiving no reply and going on to say, "Minister Kate told us not to gossip about you for dropping out of choir but that one of us should reach out to you if you're backsliding."

That disclosure smarted. Nikkita's eyes narrowed. "Is that what this conversation is, then? Outreach?"

"What? No, no," Ian took less than a second to answer. "That's not what I—"

"Is somebody gonna win a big box of gumdrops and gift cards if they get me to come back to church?" A rhetorical question misdirected, Nikkita knew, but Ian was the only youth group member on the other side of the phone call.

He didn't respond right away. When he did, his voice was lower. "I shouldn't have said anything about them. This isn't about them." Distress was evident in the sigh he released. "Come on, Nikki. Talk to me. Did I do something?"

"No." Another shot of pain and guilt. Nikkita sucked in a breath at the twinge. "No, don't think that. It's..." Her mind scrambled for an answer, pouncing down on the first one she came up with. "Maybe I never really stopped being the new girl there. Kind of an outsider."

"What? Still?"

More scrambling. A second pounce. "I'm not one of the people the rest of you have known since kindergarten."

"So?"

She pounced again and came up with nothing.

"Okay. Okay." Ian's next words were slow. Weighed down. "Well, can I just see you, then? Can I come over tomorrow, or something?"

Oh... Of course he would ask that. What was more, before too long, if her parents started making curious comments about however many weeks it'd been since Ian's last visit,

Nikkita might wind up stretching her "senioritis watch" and "not hanging out as much" excuses pretty thin.

Ian's voice was anxious, strained, when he met her silence with another try. "I really want to see you."

Yes. Yes he did, no doubt.

It took her standing up to a flood of longing—a flood of IMs and text messages and rec room music sessions and *Beaver* episodes and special weekend trips to a soda fountain and laughter and tears and shared looks full of knowing—it took standing up to that and more for Nikkita to tell Ian, "That wouldn't be a good idea." She dropped down to a mumble. "We probably wouldn't ever see each other again anyway, after I leave for college."

Although she was standing up to the flood, she couldn't stop it from flowing through the phone.

"Never see each other again?" Ian asked with the pitch of someone being flooded. Quietly drowning. "Why would you even say that?"

Nikkita forced a groan, weak as it was. "I know people sometimes think like their high school friendships will last forever, but most of them don't. People grow up and move away and life goes on—"

"This is me, Nikkita. Me and you."

If she told herself she couldn't hear the tremble in Ian's voice, she'd be lying.

"Me and you," he said, "so why don't you want to see me?" More than a request for an explanation, that question of his was a plea.

Nikkita gritted her teeth to prevent her own trembling. She wasn't entirely successful, but it only took one more pounce by her. Pouncing on a point of defense Ian hadn't meant to hand over to her that way.

"You wouldn't want to backslide with me," she asserted, her voice holding off a breakdown just long enough to tell him, "So, please...it's better if you leave me alone. Okay?"

No. It was anything but okay. For that reason, Nikkita ended the phone call before Ian could tell her so.

And before he could hear her begin to weep.

Chapter Seven

"I JUST...I MISS US, Nikki. You know?"

Here, driving down the streets of this all-too-familiar town in her crossover vehicle, she had two more turns to go.

She took them, pulling into the far side of the parking lot of a new business establishment, which wasn't open yet at this early hour of the morning.

Nikkita parked, got out of her crossover, closed the vehicle's door, and leaned back against it, folding her arms. As she stared over at the building near the center of the property, her mind slid back to much that she'd gradually learned in past years, piece by piece, through a few connections of hers on social media.

Shortly after Nikkita's departure for college, news about Pastor Tyler and Jayme leaked into the church. The leak came along with news about Pastor Tyler and another teenage girl at the church. Sandra.

The church leadership board conducted in-house questioning through a series of separate meetings with different members of the church. The meetings revealed that at various times in the years since the church had hired him on, Pastor Tyler might have carried on sexual relationships with at least five girls while they were in the youth ministry.

"You were next on his list, apparently," Jayme had mumbled to Nikkita during one of their rare check-up conversations over the phone, back when Nikkita was nearing her graduation from college. "Who knew he had a list? I didn't." Jayme let out a gravelly sound that might have been a laugh. "Because he told me I was different, I was stupid enough to think I was his only one. When Sandra started pushing to get me to stop seeing him all of a sudden, she didn't even hint that he had something going on with her too, and the further she went trying to 'trust the process' with him was starting to scare her."

Nikkita had shaken her head at that, getting a tighter grip on her phone. "You weren't stupid, Jayme. You were conditioned and manipulated by someone who had a lot of practice at twisting things. A man you looked up to and counted on."

The in-house questioning at church never uncovered the whole picture of exactly how many girls Pastor Tyler had made advances to or drew into "unique relationships." Moreover, the church's general members remained unclear on how many of the girls and their families had been pressured into silence on the matter.

"Yeah," Sandra had eventually said on social media, in a private group of a number of people from different parts of the country who'd broken away from churches they'd once attended. "The church board met with me and my parents. The board told us that letting a scandal get out in public would hurt the body of Christ because we're supposed to have grace and cover other believers when they fall. And Pastor Paul said telling anyone about it outside of our church would ruin our witness and hinder the Gospel. So basically, if I or any other members reported what happened in our church or if we pressed charges or anything, then sinners who heard about it would probably reject Christianity, miss out on salvation, end up in hell, and we 'the scandalmongers' would be responsible for it. The whole thing was bizarre to me, how I could walk into that meeting feeling scared and used and violated, and then the board had me feeling scared and guilty by the time I walked out. Like if I'd ever want to speak up about it, I must be a selfish, bad Christian."

In due course, it came to light that part of the problem with the leadership board's questioning was the fact that the head of the board, Pastor Paul, had been in a reciprocal agreement to "cover a fallen believer," Pastor Tyler, longer than most people knew. Both men were aware of Pastor Tyler's preying on youth group girls, both men were aware of an affair Pastor Paul had been having for several years with a woman who lived on his neighborhood block, and both men had covered for each other.

Until their mutual covering no longer held up against leaking information.

Membership at the church began to shrink. A few of the church's leaders in ministry, including Minister Kate, resigned. Pastor Tyler relocated somewhere across the country, leaving the crumbling church to Pastor Paul, whose wife took some time trying to salvage the ministry with him before she finally divorced him.

The Eversons had been one of the first families to leave the church when the leaking started. After holding off for a time, Ian had looked up Nikkita on her college's website and contacted her through her school email address, saying he didn't know if Pastor Tyler was the reason she'd left the church but asking her if she was okay.

"You don't have to answer me," Ian wrote, "and I won't contact you again if you don't want me to. I just wanted to check."

Nikkita had taken a few days to reply. "Hi, Ian! Thank you for checking. Honestly, no, I'm not okay. Not about that, anyway. But school's great, and I hope it is for you too. Say hi to your mom for me. Thanks again and take care!"

It wouldn't be until much later that Nikkita would quite understand: Even as she was warmed and relieved that Ian thought of her and took the risk to get in touch with her once more, her psyche was in multifaceted crisis mode when she received his email. She then mentally kicked herself an untold number of times after she clicked "Send" on her reply message. Upon reading it, Ian would be more than able to tell he was still shut out where she was concerned.

She hated that it hurt so much to hear from someone who'd gone to that church.

Not long after that, she got a call from home one evening, both her mom and dad on the line. Ian's mom had contacted Nikkita's parents and said they should talk to their daughter in case something had happened to her at church.

"No, no, I never went to his office," Nikkita wasted no time in answering her parents' inquiry that night. "I was fine just talking to him when he stopped by our choir rehearsals. We talked about school and stuff."

She grew unnervingly hot while trying to be selective in her sharing of details. "He came off as friendly and pastory all the time, but no, I never met with him alone, and he never tried to reach me after I stopped going to church. So you don't have to worry. Please."

After that night, a significant part of her spent a period of time wishing she could block that season of her life from her memory.

All the same, here she was now, standing in a parking lot where simmering memories, almost palpable in their presence, had followed her out of her crossover.

Since Nikkita had been gone from this town, more than one business had moved on and off the property where she now stood: the property that had been converted into a new car dealership, at which she wasn't looking to buy a car. She continued staring toward the dealership's main building.

The church that had once been here, the one Nikkita had first attended on a youth Outreach Nite, was no more.

Chapter Eight

AFTER NIKKITA'S PARENTS reached retirement, the two of them moved out of state and bought a smaller house where they'd be closer to both their families. Before then, between the start of Nikkita's adult years and the start of her parents' retirement years, she would see her mom and dad when they all met for out-of-town family get-togethers with everyone. So, her parents wouldn't have been the reason for Nikkita to stop by this town today instead of simply going straight to the next county as the members of her band would be doing.

Most times when she was on the road for a reason outside of her music career, it was indeed for family get-togethers, whether she was going off for a stay in one of their homes or she'd scheduled to meet up with cousins of hers somewhere for a group getaway. A few incidents arose when amorous men invited Nikkita on getaways of a different kind, but while she did a moderate share of dating on and off, she didn't go on any romantic vacations.

The people she kept up with online still included Jayme, now a single mother who had a career in social work, doing all she could to find safe foster homes for children rescued from abusive living situations. Most of Nikkita's time online was for her own business purposes, though, what with her vlog and news about her music releases and live performances.

Even so, she'd gotten back in touch with Ian online after her college years. She sent a nervous request to connect with him on social media; he accepted her request the same day. She took it as a positive sign that he didn't hate her for shutting him out several years before, but they exchanged no private messages.

Like two distant acquaintances, they mostly kept their interaction to liking or laughing at some of each other's social media posts, except whenever Nikkita announced she had new music available. On those occasions, Ian would make more noise, being one of the first to come and express enthusiasm on her announcements, and he'd always come back later to say which of the songs topped his playlist. Nikkita would thank him for it, love it, and try not to love it too much.

She'd wait, breathe, and do her best to keep it together while scrolling down the screen of her devices sometimes to see everyday pictures that Ian posted.

Pictures of him with his mom, in between trips she'd started taking with a group of globetrotters who were in or nearing their autumn years. Pictures of Ian with his sister and the growing brood of children she had with her boyfriend. Pictures of Ian with his friends. Pictures of Ian with his wife.

A willowy, red-haired woman he'd met in college. Kelsey.

Nikkita had literally laughed out loud—a choking laugh, but a laugh nonetheless—when she'd first seen a particular wedding picture of Ian and Kelsey's. He in his tux but without the jacket. She in her gown but without the veil. Both of them in sneakers. Kelsey somehow managing to sit piggyback on a stooped Ian, a jokey yet radiant smile beaming from her while Ian's face feigned agony at the camera, like a man on the verge of being crushed beneath the weight of his slim and lithe wife.

"It's because that fancy dress of hers weighed a ton and three quarters," Ian had qualified in his comment above the picture.

Kelsey had jumped on to leave a reply. "Don't believe his hogwash, folks. My new hubby was being a poor sport. We were playing leapfrog, he stood up too fast and wasn't ready, and I got stuck up there."

On certain days, Nikkita couldn't handle scrolling through the sweet, lovely, and comical depictions of Ian's married life. Other times, she let her curiosity have free rein as she'd smile or chuckle at one Everson post or another, a peculiar knot of anticipation twisting within her while she waited to one day scroll upon evidence that Ian and Kelsey had started raising a family.

Every now and then, Ian posted about his work as a new home sales consultant for a custom homebuilder. "Bring me your dream, and I'll help you live in it," he'd say, sharing sponsored posts with pictures of modern, spacious, energy-efficient homes built by the company he worked for.

Yet, there came a time when the frequency of Ian's posting began to lessen, after he shared that Kelsey was dealing with heart failure. His personal posting then became almost nonexistent after Kelsey passed away.

That tragedy had happened about a year and a half ago.

Kelsey hadn't wanted a large funeral. In accordance with the instructions she'd given before her passing, Ian saw to it that a prewritten request of hers was sent out in private messages and emails to the people the Everson couple knew.

Hi there, friends, fam, and friends of fam!

My absolutely phenomenal hubs and I agreed that he can use all the casseroles and home-baked brownies you bring him, for those of you who are local to us. But please, everyone—no building any golden death shrines for me.

That is, don't take grief so far that you start thinking and talking and acting like dying is the biggest thing I ever did. I trust that most of you know me better than that.

My expenses are already taken care of, so if you want to honor my heavenly elevation in monetary fashion, promote life! Please send a donation to one of the following research hospitals and health associations working to find cures for serious diseases.

And no, I didn't go grab a bunch of random charity names off the internet in a last-minute rush to do something noble. (Ha!)

These are all charities I've vetted and have personally partnered with in some capacity over the years. I've got all the donation links listed for you below this spiel of mine. (See? Did you stop to peek down at 'em?)

Oodles of thanks, everyone, and I'm looking forward to seeing you all on the other side.

So much love,

Kels

A shaky, amazed sigh streamed through Nikkita's lips after she reread the main request from Ian's wife. *Faith, hope, and charity. And the greatest of these...*

Nikkita made a donation and also sent a letter with her personal condolences to Ian before she went back to past posts of his on social media one day, scrolling through. Smiling here. Chuckling there. Wincing at the sweetness, the loveliness, the loving comedy displayed through what had begun as the chronicles of a husband and had become the memories of a widower.

Ian.

I'm sorry.

I'm so sorry.

The ache within Nikkita consisted of multiple layers, which collectively kept her from taking the liberty, taking the step that Ian eventually did. About a year after Nikkita had sent him her condolence letter, he was the one to reinitiate contact with her. Not merely for them to keep to social media this time, but they got back to text messaging each other. Video chatting also became a mode of communication for them at times when Nikkita wasn't on the road. She found talking through the screen of her tablet to be more comfortable than "voice without a face" talks over the phone.

For months, their conversations generally weren't too long or deep. Nikkita kept her sharing on the light side, concerned about stepping or leaning on any areas that might yet be tender or excruciating for someone who'd experienced losses like Ian's.

Still, it was via video chat one night at her apartment when Nikkita finally gave Ian a basic account of what happened to her back on the day she left their old church as a high school senior, along with certain overtures and actions that had led up to it.

She also expressed regret for the way she'd parted from Ian. "I should've told you I was sorry ages ago, but I wasn't sure if it'd be a 'too little, too late' move you'd only find insulting by then."

Ian's gaze averted from her expression, his hand going up to rake through his hair. "You weren't responsible for...for that whole thing," he said.

Nikkita shook her head. "I'm not apologizing for that whole thing but for the way I hurt you." The grimace that passed over his face sent a pang through her, discouraging her from going on, but she tried to anyway. "I didn't know how else to handle it at the time, but I..."

Ian went silent long enough for Nikkita to suspect he'd have no more to say. When his eyes came back to the screen of her propped-up tablet and he did speak, his words took her off guard. "We can figure out how to handle more than this now, though. Right?" He waved a hand between the two of them. "More than what we've been doing these past months?"

His question landed right where it was meant to. She knew it but made the cautious choice to feel him out about it instead of plunging headlong into anything. "What do you mean?"

Ian sat there, exhaled, and answered. "See, the way Kelsey went didn't come as any shock to me."

Oh...? Not a shock to him. But a new, unexpected piece of information for Nikkita.

"She was open about her health and medical history from the time she and I got serious," Ian went on, "especially because of how I lost my dad. I had it out with her, and we both agreed we were worth it. Being together for any length of time she and I might have would be worth it, and we actually had more years than I sometimes thought we would." His eyes leveled on Nikkita's as steadily as they could over a camera. "So much better than if she and I had been spending our lives just as friends, wishing every day for more than that."

Nikkita stared at him, his statement dropping, splashing through her guarded surface like a mass of rock broken from a mountain, sending much more than a ripple through her. Feeling him out about this any further wouldn't be necessary for Nikkita, but Ian had only gotten started.

He'd reinitiated communication between them those months ago, and now he'd gotten started.

"I know it's been years for you and me," Ian told her next, "and we've lived a lot of life away from each other. It's obviously different now than it was then. At the same time, I just..." He brought up a searching hand, seeking out the words. "I miss us, Nikki. You know?"

Her mouth opened in silence. She knew.

And it had been about two decades since the last time she'd heard him call her that.

"I'm not even talking about the teenage version of us so much," Ian made the effort to explain, "even though, hey. We were the best thing around back then." His own boasting drew a half-smile out of him, and she matched the smile before it faded away. "But what about who we should be now?" he asked. "Don't get me wrong—I feel blessed that we're even in contact with each other, after everything. But this nice and polite way we've been going about it, leaving so much unsaid..." He shook his head. "This isn't us."

No. No, it wasn't. Not really.

After a moment, Ian looked downward, scratching at his forehead. "I miss us," he reiterated on a quiet note, said no more for a while, and then lifted his eyes back to Nikkita. "Don't you?"

She didn't need him to ask her that question twice.

Hence, here she was this morning, having completed her visit to the dealership where her old church used to be. She was again driving through the streets of this place she didn't refer to as her hometown, heading for a baseball field at which there wasn't any game scheduled for the day.

Her destination would mostly be empty, given its location at a high school and the fact that, despite the way the weather here was clinging to the milder feel of spring, high school baseball season was over and school was out for the summer.

Yet, the high school in question was the one Ian had attended as a student. When Nikkita recently told him she could swing by this town along the way to the last stop on her current tour, the two of them agreed to meet at this baseball field.

She saw a lone figure in the bleachers when she pulled up to the nearby parking lot. They were the bleachers where she used to sit, stand, and cheer at Ian's home games. By the time she took a drink from a large water bottle she had with her, stuffed the bottle into her tote bag, and got out of her crossover to begin making her way toward the bleachers, Ian had already come down, standing with his hands parked in the pockets of his jeans.

Sure, Nikkita had seen all of those posted pictures of him over the years. The two of them had seen each other over their video chats. But it was something else altogether to be approaching him in person after all this time, a man now as close to the threshold of middle age as she was.

It was something to see in person that his thick, dark hair—which he still wore a little long on top but now with a smooth, dignified wave styled into it—had some strands that had gone gray after he lost his wife. From the fall of his casual but sharp button-up over his husky frame, it was apparent that his shirt designed to be worn untucked didn't have a washboard concealed underneath it.

While outfits like Nikkita's light top with fluttery bell sleeves and her straight-leg jeans were helpful complements for her pear shape, her hips were even more ample than they used to be. Also, although she'd gotten the best sleep that she and her overactive thoughts could manage the night before, she knew she didn't look to be at her most rested.

Yet, what were a relatively restless night, added pounds, gray hairs, and nearly twenty years gone by? What were they in light of the reality that she was walking toward this man now, and he, after giving her a smile, dipped his head, dropped his shoulders, and let out a laugh?

It wasn't the loudest or longest laugh Nikkita had ever heard from Ian, but with all the weight that seemed to roll from his shoulders with the release of it, she couldn't say she'd ever heard a sound from him that was more relieving. Or more joyous.

Nikkita had thrown the strap of her tote over her shoulder when she'd gotten out of her vehicle, but seconds from now, that fashionable accessory of hers would be in the way if she let it. It wasn't her most ladylike move to allow her tote to slip from her shoulder and to thump down to a patch of grass at her sandaled feet, and Ian didn't make the gentlemanly move to stoop down and retrieve her fallen property for her.

There was little time for anything like that at the moment. As soon as Ian's hands were free of his pockets and his arms were out to receive her, Nikkita moved right into them, her own hands going behind him to clasp the back of his shoulders.

Their embrace wasn't a short one. Ian brought his head to rest against Nikkita's, and her eyes slipped to a close as her being savored the strength of Ian's arms around her. A strength under control but no less evident.

Minutes came and went before any words passed between the two of them. Even then, their embrace didn't come to an end. Ian had but to angle his head the slightest bit to allow his warm whisper to be heard perfectly through the curly layers of Nikkita's hair.

"Hey, Nik-Nik."

A smile touched her lips, but her eyes didn't open, her head having no need to turn and her whisper equally as warm as it floated from her mouth.

"Hello, Bean."

Chapter Nine

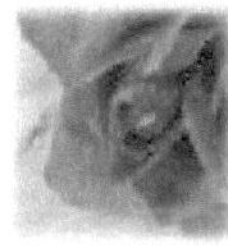

SITTING TOGETHER IN the bleachers at the baseball field, they didn't pass the morning away with small talk. They both knew that to wade in a pleasantry pool wasn't her reason for taking a detour from her tour or his reason to be here during vacation time he was taking from his job.

"I couldn't understand why you didn't tell me," Ian was saying now. "I mean, I know the board pressured Jayme and Sandra and whoever else to keep quiet, and it'd been ingrained in us for years to obey our church leaders. You were gone before those meetings with the board happened, though."

"Ah. Well." Nikkita let out a hard, short sigh. "I think I'm like a lot of people who face stuff like this, with so many different reasons for keeping quiet. Once you expose your painful business, it's at the mercy of other people." She held out her hands, palms upward, weighing them back and forth. "You start to wonder, 'If I tell, will the person who did this to me try to get revenge? What if people don't believe me, or they say I brought it on myself? Or that I'm making a big deal out of nothing? Will they wind up excusing the person who did it and leave me to pick up the pieces?' I could think up a host of different reasons, and I'm only one person." She dropped her hands. "Sandra says she left her meeting with the church board feeling like she didn't have a right to tell anyone else. I get how she felt that way."

Ian gave half a nod at her mention of Sandra, but then the lines on his brow deepened.

Nikkita was circling above the crux of an answer for the personal question he'd asked without asking. She wasn't quite able to land yet, but she pushed ahead, determined to make her way there.

"It can be hard when you're facing someone in a position of power. Influence," she said, the fingers of one of her hands curling. Clenching. "When Pastor Tyler made his move on me that day, instinct would've had me punch him in the face. But I saw myself as still pretty new to faith, and he was known as a man of God. If I told on him, what if he had a way to convince other people that I'd misconstrued everything? Or if he flat-out denied that anything had happened, it would be my word against his." She loosened her hand to relieve her knuckles. "Who would enough people at that church have been more likely to stand beside? An established leader they admired, a man they'd learned to trust for years, or the different little new girl?"

A dim light of recognition flashed in Ian's eyes. He didn't attempt to hand her one answer or another she wasn't truly asking him to give her.

One of Nikkita's hands came up toward her ear for a second, making the sign of a phone. "Finding out about him and Jayme didn't make me feel like my story would be more believable, or believable enough. He'd sweet-talked her up and deluded her for so long and she was so spellbound, it seemed to me she'd probably lie for him to the church if she felt she had to. Or if I told her he'd tried to seduce me, maybe she'd see me as competition and do her best to shove me out of the picture. I didn't know.

"Either way..." Nikkita came near to absently rubbing a certain spot on her thigh, but she realized it and stopped herself. "While it was happening that day, the unsure side of me was like, 'Do I even have a right to stand up to "a man of God"?'" She emphasized that label with a slight inflection before she brushed it to the side. "I know now that of course I did, but in the moment, I froze. All mixed-up. With this strange kind of fear."

Another dim flash passed through Ian's eyes. "Deer in headlights?" he offered.

Nikkita accepted that with resignation. "It might sound trite, but the effect is a real thing." She snatched the air before her in a quick, tight grip. "The freeze-up."

Ian's head moved pensively up and down at that, and he asked, "What happened after you ran out of choir practice?"

Nikkita let go of the air. "I didn't go home right away. One or both my parents might've decided to hang around the house for the afternoon and would wonder about me coming back too early. I drove around, parked at the library but didn't go in." She shook her head toward one lifting shoulder. "I delayed and wound up not saying anything to my parents that day. They already weren't rah-rah-rah about the church, and I was especially afraid of what my dad might do. I got these images of him going into full-on 'defend my baby girl' mode and doing something to land himself in jail."

A grave grunt from Ian indicated his identifying with that, the rigid ring of conviction sounding from his throat.

"Besides," Nikkita hurried on, "what I heard from Jayme left me so horrified, I just wanted to disappear from the situation." Her forehead scrunched, and she gathered the fingertips of one hand together, holding them up to her temple. "You find out about grievous stuff going on in church"—her fingertips popped apart, an invisible bubble bursting—"and it can make you question everything they taught you to believe."

Ian let out a heavy puff of breath, his head shaking but with concurrence. "It can. I had to do some messy reevaluating myself." He looked out toward the baseball field, his hand indicating unseen points of the past. "What were their angles when they preached this or that to us? How much of what sounded right to me at one time was right, and how much was actually twisted teaching?" Both his hands then came together and separated like a book breaking apart. "How much of my own Bible reading was skewed by ideas I first absorbed in church without knowing those ideas were off?"

The understanding Nikkita shared with him on that score wasn't satisfying for her. Still, she... "I had a hard time sorting through it all after being there less than three years." Satisfying or not, she felt compelled to make sure he knew she understood this much: "You'd been going to that church all your life."

Ian squinted toward the field, his jaw stirring with a stiff roll, and his gaze returned to Nikkita. "I don't remember when Pastor Tyler showed up. There was a different youth pastor before, but I was in the children's ministry with the children's pastor and wasn't paying attention to who every other leader was yet."

He waved a hand, dismissing those incomplete details. "But yes, Pastor Paul had been the senior pastor as long as I could remember, and people don't end up running down blatantly corrupt paths without taking any wrong steps to get there. I can't help wondering what his steps were. How much more went on behind closed doors at our church that we didn't know about? No one who wasn't behind every door knows everything he was doing or allowing back there, or how many people were involved. Or for how long."

Ian's eyebrows lowered, heat seeping into his voice. "It still gets me under the collar to think that Pastor Paul was the one who gave the eulogy at my dad's service. Up there in his pulpit, preaching on true manhood and family and faithfulness. Maybe not meaning any of it the way he said it, but standing there proclaiming it over the casket anyway. As if he was in such manly solidarity with the dead." One of Ian's hands came up in a fist, thumping against his heart. "*My* dead."

Nikkita cringed. Likely the foremost funeral in Ian's memory for most of his life. A memory stained.

She hadn't thought about that aspect of the overall issue.

"It took years and going through a few different churches Kelsey and I didn't feel right about before we settled on the one we...the one I go to now," Ian went on. "Besides that it's almost an hour-long drive from home, I can't name major downsides to it." His look turned rueful. "But I guess I can tell you, in a corner of my mind, I haven't gotten past waiting to maybe...find out something about the place. At some point or another."

Nikkita's slight smile was a downhearted one. "Something behind a closed door?"

Ian's lips imitated hers without exactly smiling back. "I pray I won't feel this way forever. It might just take a little more time. Time to find some trust." He hesitated, silently shifting course before taking the chance to budge himself, gently bumping Nikkita's knee with his. "I wasn't sure if you trusted me enough to come back here." When her eyebrows lifted somewhat, he added, "For a visit."

She went still before responding to the knee-bump in kind with good humor, but her look was somber. And sorry. "Ian. When I didn't tell you what happened to me back then, it wasn't that I thought *you* wouldn't believe me or anything."

Upon hearing that, Ian inclined his head a searching degree toward her, his tone treading lightly. "Then what was it?"

Where was Nikkita with her circling above the crux she had yet to reach for him? She hadn't come here today to leave a part of him in the dark.

Because her mouth threatened to dry out, she didn't start explaining until after she'd turned to her tote beside her, fetched out her water, and took a drink. "Well." She put the water away and turned back to Ian. "Even with me and you being me and you, I was humiliated. Afraid to face you," she confessed, and the measure of bewildered concern that came over Ian's face made her swift in pressing forward. "See, you remember those sermons we used to hear on sexual purity, right?"

Ian's head turned a tad to one side. "Right..." The word hung at a wary angle.

"Right." Nikkita didn't dig her heels in beneath her but the balls of her feet instead, as if in preparation for an upward climb. "The way the pastors would drive home warnings on the need for women's modesty would leave me with this icky, heavy feeling." She flickered her fingers near her person, suggesting a sticky residue. "The way they'd tell us, 'Men are so easily turned on by what they see. So modesty, modesty, ladies. So that you don't tempt the men who may be looking at you.' And Minister Kate and some of the moms at church told us girls to only hug guys from the side, *if* we had to hug them at all."

Nikkita's arms moved in the brief motion of a noncommittal embrace. "Stuff like that gave the impression that women's bodies must be shameful. Our bodies must be catalysts for sin, since the way we're made is apparently such a dangerous thing for men."

Ian's eyes didn't leave her, but it seemed that was due to an uneasy effort.

"The things they said didn't even address the reality that not all men are attracted to women," Nikkita continued, "or only to women. But our pastors' sermons never warned the men in the congregation about, say, wearing sexy cowboy jeans. Or men going swimming out in public, getting all wet while they're wearing nothing but clingy trunks covering less than half their bodies. 'Modesty, modesty, gentlemen.' Those sermons never said that." She indicated Ian with one hand. "And did anyone at church ever tell you to lay off from hugging other guys or to only give them a quick squeeze from the side, in case something might happen?"

Ian gave a clipped, humorless laugh. "I can't say they did."

"Didn't think so. They didn't talk about men's bodies as if they're shameful or dangerous because some men may be so easily turned on by seeing them or hugging them." Nikkita's hand went to her chest. "But we women were called out in church, advised to manage our looks in a way that would supposedly guard men. Keep them from getting turned on. If a guy ever came on to me or had to struggle not to, then it was up to me to improve my level of modesty. Otherwise, it was basically my fault for allowing him to be urged by my dangerous body." Her eyes narrowed as she lifted a finger to tap at her ear through her hair. "That's what those sermons sounded like.

"Then what happened after all those warnings to the ladies?" Nikkita jerked a thumb to the side. "The man leading the youth ministry came on to me. While I agonized over it after that day, it seemed like it had to be my fault, since a man ordained to the service of God wouldn't just *do* something like that."

Having not anticipated her voice becoming quivery, she swallowed against the feeling, straightening her shoulders for a delivery of old hypotheticals, once hashed and rehashed in her past. "Maybe I'd smiled at Pastor Tyler the wrong way. Maybe I shouldn't have worn makeup, or should have worn baggier clothes. Maybe I shouldn't have tried out for any more solos in the choir after the first time, when I saw that he was moved by my singing."

She directed her hand around a corner. "During prayer times at choir rehearsals, maybe I'd done the wrong thing by letting him pray with me around the corner of the sound booth, where the rest of the room couldn't quite see us. Was I asking for it when I kept sitting in my favorite spot to pray in the sanctuary?"

Nikkita wasn't doing the best job of keeping the quivers at bay. Even if she couldn't hear that reality, the downcast response of Ian's eyes would've tipped her off to it.

Her past hypotheticals persisted, quivers and all. "Maybe his coming over and finding me there in the first place was a spiritual test, and I'd failed. I knew he wasn't married, didn't have a wife to keep his urges satisfied, as he and Pastor Paul preached that wives would." She spread her hands in wide, declarative fashion before an unseen congregation of believing listeners. "Pastor Paul was especially good at it, praising his wife so well to all of us while he was cheating on her." The unseen congregation vanished, and she lowered her hands. "That aside, my teenage brain hadn't reached the point to consider that marriage wasn't the kind of cure-all they sometimes made it sound like."

Nikkita then came to a pause. Her psyche took the opportunity to remind her that she, a woman who'd never been to the altar, was speaking to a man who'd been not only to the altar but also to the cemetery.

It seemed to take a beat or two for Nikkita's pause to register with Ian. He observed her for a while and said, "No, I...I get it." He signaled for her to go on. "I'm listening."

Yes. He was.

After telling herself to stay mindful of him, Nikkita went on. "So. When Pastor Tyler kept visiting me around the booth, maybe I'd failed in my feminine duty to guard him. To tell him to go away, so that he wouldn't be there struggling with too strong an urge to touch me and the reminder of no wife to go home to. I'd once assumed his knowing me by name and checking on me must have been a good thing, a right thing, because of who he was." She gave an empty gesture at the thought of where that assumption had gone.

Even so, the mention of it had given her the lead she needed to finish circling a related stretch of landscape surrounding all of this and to finally land.

She held Ian's gaze with hers, lowering her voice. "Outside of the men in my family, I'd gotten closer to you than any other guy I knew. Our friendship felt like a good thing. A right thing. But if I'd been wrong about one male/female association I'd first thought was right, maybe I also could have been wrong about my friendship with you."

Ian only sat there for a moment before his shoulders sagged in unmistakable deflation. "Nikki."

She almost didn't hear the name, given the deep moan that enclosed it.

Nikkita carried her explanation forward, lest she should be tempted to drop it while standing still with the weight of it. "I thought that maybe as dangerous as I was for Tyler, I was for you. Maybe it'd be sinful of me to stay close to you, and it was my feminine duty to end it. To guard you."

When Ian's mouth opened as if to protest, Nikkita reached for him, placing a hand on his forearm, needing him to hear her. "You had college right ahead of you, Ian. An adult life to prepare for." Her free hand took a second to grab and turn an unseen steering wheel. "You needed direction. Not distractions. And Tyler had convinced me of how much of a bad, distracting temptation I could be."

She ended her touch on Ian's arm so that both her hands could go back to her chest. "If there was something about me, and if my presence became too much—more than even a dedicated *pastor* could stand—then what would make me think I could be a safe place for a teenage guy full of teenage hormones?"

"But I never even..." Ian's hands came up in what was yet a plain, troubled need for protest. "I mean, of course I, um, thought about you. You were my best girl and I was mad into you, but we knew that already and we never—"

"No," Nikkita softly interrupted. Her heart took no more than a secret second to bask in the boyish description of Ian's younger self concerning her, and perhaps the mix of centuries in his attempt to make sense of those feelings through English. "No, nothing like that had happened between us before," she said. "And I'm more aware now of the difference between really being into someone, appreciating their appeal, versus objectifying someone, where they're less of a person in your eyes or hardly a person at all. You never made me feel like I was less than me to you." She paused to let that affirmation sink in. "But the point was that after Tyler showed me that I must be dangerous, I imagined something *could* go wrong between me and you if I didn't prevent it."

Ian's hands lingered in protest before they came down, but he looked no less disturbed.

"So," Nikkita told him, "when you brought up Minister Kate's suggestion that I might be backsliding, I thought it'd be better to let you think that's what I was doing. To keep you at a distance and protect you from me." She gave a nod of admission. "Yes, my thinking was off. I was confused.

Ashamed. Scared to death, in a way." The first finger of each of her hands came up, pointing back and forth to her ears. "After being preached to with forked tongues, my mind was a mess."

Ian drew in a breath, his shoulders straightening out of their sagging position. He released his breath and slowly nodded to her. He was listening.

Nikkita's hands took a break in her lap. "While I battled with myself, trying to pinpoint what I and Jayme had done to cause Tyler's behavior, I thought it had to be that she and I weren't careful or modest enough. Because 'modesty, modesty, ladies' was touted like..." Her mind hunted for the words. "Touted like the way for ladies to manage men's feelings. The way to keep a man from wanting to do something wrong to a woman."

More than Nikkita's hands needed a break. She stopped to look beyond the baseball field, her senses taking in the sights and sounds of a town heading toward its afternoon phase of activity. She had further to go, though, and she looked back at Ian.

"Eventually," she said, "I had to think about different places and cultures that you could say are much more careful than we are. Places where men and women live fairly separate lives, not mixing as much as we do. I thought about places and cultures where people drape themselves in loose cloth, including places where women's faces are covered." She passed a hand over her face, her eyes narrowing again, her voice firm as it dropped. "Well, even in such socially strict, careful environments, sexual abuse and assault, rape—it all still happens in those places."

Ian grimaced but didn't turn away from her stare.

"And here I'd been," Nikkita said, her hand becoming a fist to rest down on her hip, "wondering if it was because I didn't follow Minister Kate's instruction to wear sports bras to church, and wondering if it was my makeup and girly jeans that had driven a man to touch me. Because, according to his preaching, if I'd been more careful and if he'd gotten better modesty from me, he would have stayed—"

"Would have stayed focused on the things of God."

At first, Nikkita was taken aback when Ian filled in that piece with her. Yet, he remembered those sermons as well, as he'd said he did.

"Focused on the things of God," Nikkita took her time in repeating, "instead of working out a strategy for seducing a girl in his ministry. During my years of trying to sort through everything after that, I had to come back to certain ideas with fresh eyes."

A preliminary grunt got away from her at the irony. Preliminary in relation to where she was going next, as she told herself that since she'd already stepped out here, she might as well go all the way there.

"Eyes," she said again, pointing near the corners of each of her eyelids. "If your right eye makes you sin, pluck it out. Isn't that what Jesus said?"

Ian's own eyes popped wider at her mention of that, but he didn't appear lost. "It is."

"So it is." Nikkita's fingertip tapped at her temple. "Even if He was speaking metaphorically, I had to look at a principle there." She pointed out toward the ball field, but not the ball field. "I didn't see it saying, 'Go deal with the thing over there, the thing your eye is looking at. That's where the problem is.'"

Her finger abandoned the ball field to point to herself. "What I saw it saying was 'Dig out whatever's in you that makes you sin. Deal with *you*.'"

Nikkita's hands drew out the form of a female figure in the air. "Jesus didn't say there that if a man looks at a woman and lusts for her, it's her duty to guard the man by toning down her appeal, to try to become more shapeless and colorless in her appearance. Jesus also didn't say the man there must be lusting after the woman because he doesn't have a wife, or that if he does"—Nikkita again used her voice to make a specific inflection—"the man's wife must not be 'fulfilling her role' to satisfy him."

Ian didn't have to reach for a past message from their old church for the next piece he filled in with a musing murmur. "If a man looks at a woman and lusts for her, he's already committed adultery."

Nikkita nodded at that. "It says he's committed adultery in his heart. The verse doesn't point to the woman there as if she's a problem in need of controlling or fixing because a man looked at her and felt something he shouldn't. It's the lust he's got in *his* heart that's the problem. He hasn't plucked out his objectifying eye. He hasn't dealt with himself."

When she saw what looked to be a tense bobbing of Ian's Adam's apple, Nikkita let her gaze fall. She brushed at her jeans in preoccupation. "I don't think there's something wrong with holding modesty as a value, though not everyone shares the same concepts about modesty and immodesty." She wiped a piece of lint or pollen from her knee. "I mean, hey, it may be possible that cultures and tribes where certain nudity isn't inherently sexual or considered offensive, where the women live as freely bare-chested as the men do—in that way, they might be living in a purer state like in the Garden of Eden, where God's children lived naked and without shame."

An abrupt choking sound escaped Ian, and he cleared his throat.

Looking up to find him blushing, Nikkita gave him a small smile of reassurance. "Don't worry. I'm all for wearing clothes." She lifted her arms to create a butterfly effect with her bell sleeves. "Especially cute ones." Her arms settled smoothly to give her sleeves a flowing landing. "And especially in cold weather. Can't deny that being all covered up isn't a bad idea when an arctic chill blows in."

Ian chuckled, his hand going up to scratch at his reddened cheek.

After chuckling with him, Nikkita didn't take long in growing serious again. "But now, here on the other side of what I've been through, I see that I'm not for pushing modesty as a demand on women because of men's urges or lust." She opened her hands. "Of course, men aren't the only ones who have lustful thoughts, so in that scenario about a man looking at a woman, I see a greater principle." She ran the fingers of one hand down her opposite palm, skimming a page without looking at it. "A principle about people needing to deal with what's in their own hearts. To deal with the way they think about what they see."

Ian's head gave a few pondering nods. "Makes sense."

Nikkita closed her invisible book. "The principle made even more sense to me once I learned that it isn't sexual urges that drive people to abuse or rape other people. Humans aren't wild animals, and libido doesn't make you go out and assault somebody." She pointed back in the general direction of the church that was no more, acid climbing up her throat. "It wasn't libido that made Tyler grope me and get girls to come to his office. It's the lust for dominance and control that drives abusers. They get this twisted sense that they have a right to—"

Cutting herself off when the acid didn't leave right away, Nikkita took a moment to calm herself before saying, "Anyway. That's stuff I had to talk about with a counselor."

Ian hesitated for a second and spoke up. "You went to counseling about this?"

"I did. While I was in college. At the same time I was taking guitar lessons on the side too." Nikkita could only make an imaginary strum at strings, since Rosa was resting back in the crossover. "It wasn't easy to keep up with it all, but it helped."

Setting her thought of Rosa aside, Nikkita sighed. "I had to learn to see through fresh eyes before I could realize and accept that what Tyler did to me wasn't my fault." She swallowed past a bad taste in her mind. "For too long after his sermons, 'healing' was a tainted word to me. Once I'd stopped blaming myself and healed enough to articulate most of this, to tell you exactly why I pulled away from you..." Her eyes offered Ian a sensitive smile in an effort to soften any potential blow. "By that time, you had Kelsey."

Rather than his cheeks, Ian's eyes were what reddened this time.

Nikkita's voice sank to a near whisper. "You weren't far from town when our old church fell apart. I knew you had to have already heard so much, and I figured it'd be late for me to dump my side of it on you. Thought it best for me to let you be. Let you be happy. And you were happy with her."

When it seemed Ian's countenance was on the cusp of crumbling, he blinked hard, gathering himself. "Very."

Nikkita let his low, loving confirmation breathe for a minute, then she infused a bit of mischief into her smile. "She must've got your bad jokes." That brought a hint of a laugh out of Ian as he looked away into the distance, and Nikkita took a chance at a question she chose a lighthearted attitude for. "Did you get the ball rolling with her in college by asking her out for a soda?"

Ian's gaze came back to Nikkita, his expression so blank that she sobered in an instant, wondering if she'd possibly offended him.

The reply he gave her was a measured one. "I didn't do sodas with her."

Nikkita went motionless, except for her mouth, which wandered open with no words to fill it.

"Or watch *Leave It to Beaver*, for that matter," Ian added, shrugging into a concise but inevitable explanation. "I wouldn't have given her an engagement ring I'd originally picked out for someone else either, if it'd come to that." His hands picked up something only he could see, setting it not aside but apart as he stared back off into the distance. "She and I had other things. Things just for me and her."

Like someone who belatedly realized they'd stepped onto hallowed ground, Nikkita let her soul step back, and she waited.

Ian used the time she allowed him, letting the air shift between them, and he spoke after the shift. "It is clearer to me now. About why you didn't tell me, back when he—" Ian bit off the end of his sentence, and his movement was sudden when he turned back to her. "But honest to God, Nikkita, if you had..."

So sudden a move from him could have made her jump, but it didn't. Her eyes stung, and she didn't try to stop it. "I know."

Anguish was evident in the shake of Ian's head. Anguish with a shade of anger. "Talk can be cheaper than cheap, so I almost don't want to say it because I was there. Oblivious. Right at the same church with you while he...while he was preying on you. On Jayme. On however many of you. And I didn't catch a clue."

Nikkita held up a hand. "Ian, you—"

"So I hope to God it doesn't sound cheap to say it, but I would've *had* you, Nikkita." The break in Ian's voice was perhaps the splintering of anger, but a fire of its own kind still burned right at his surface. "Maybe I would've had to get past the idea of killing him or something else that, yeah, would've landed me in jail. But if I'd known what happened, I wouldn't have left you dealing with it by yourself." His reddened eyes didn't receive any remedial blinking this time. "I didn't want to be a stalker, so I left you alone when you asked me to," he told her, bringing one forearm up, bracing it across his chest. "Otherwise, I would've had you. Wouldn't have let you go."

Nikkita's view of him was beginning to liquefy. "I know," she repeated on a raspy whisper, feeling no need to fight the quivery quality to her words this time. "You wouldn't have, and you didn't. Not really." She extended her raised hand to him, nudging his forearm just enough to clear the space on his chest she was aiming for.

No cunning flirtations about melting hearts. No harboring of warped notions there that would have made him see her and treat her as less than the person she was.

Clearing that space on Ian's chest, Nikkita laid gentle claim to it, pressed her palm over it, unsure of which of their two pairs of eyes was the first to let a tear fall as she lifted her gaze to his.

"I'm still in here, aren't I?" she asked Ian, feeling, waiting.

But not needing to wait, given the steady rhythm of an answer that was already beating beneath her hand.

Chapter Ten

ALL IN GOOD TIME, SHE apologized for the spots her tears and makeup left on the shoulder of his shirt.

He waved her apology away, claiming he'd never wash this shirt again, giving his own apology for blubbering into her hair and leaving it mussed.

She told him his crying needed some work if what he'd done during the last few minutes was what he considered "blubbering," but not to worry. An emergency comb was forever ready in any purse or bag she had with her. She'd also come prepared with a travel pack of tissues today. Enough to share.

He bragged that he didn't need any tissue, thanks. He'd left the spillage from his waterworks in her hair, not on his face.

She pulled out her comb and compact and handed him a couple of tissues anyhow, telling him to get to work double-checking that those beans of his were dry.

An amused, pleased aspect came and settled over his features as he accepted the tissues, asking her what other related supplies she'd lugged along in that sack of hers.

She all but hissed at him for daring to call her stylish tote bag a sack and told him no more supplies for him.

"And sorry," she went further, smiling as she took the care of her curls in hand, "no candles."

His smile matched hers. "No vigil," he remembered aloud, adding, "We're at a ball field this time anyway, as you can see. Ball fields are for playing."

"Hm. Yeah. You've got a point, there."

Hence, a short time later, the two of them were out on the otherwise empty baseball field: Ian as multiple batters taking turns at home plate and Nikkita as the pitcher standing closer than the mound for one inning, and they switched positions for the next.

It wasn't the greatest of games. Their unseeable baseball equipment afforded their two teams all kinds of room to disagree about this or that pitch or hit or miss, and neither of them saw fit to put enough into the game to kick up dirt or to break a sweat. Nevertheless, their impromptu play served its unidentified purpose well, giving them the chance to release some energy and to let a good portion of the weight of their morning lift away from their afternoon.

Nikkita didn't swing as a third pitch from Ian flew past her. "Another wacky one like that, and I'm walkin'," she warned him.

"What're you talking about?" Ian received the ball back from his catcher and rested his gloved hand against his hip. "Nah, that was a smooth one, right down the middle. Crème filling in a sandwich cookie. And your form with that bat is atrocious, Creighton. You look like you're holding a broken tennis racket."

"Tennis schmennis."

"What's that? Are we potty-mouthing out here now?"

"Nope. But what's with the stalling, Everson? Hurry up and blow it with your next pitch so I can get my walk on."

"You wanna walk that bad, huh?" Ian tossed his ball up, caught it, and dug it into his glove. "Okay. Fine. Then let's walk."

Although he hadn't given up his playful posture, more than a playful note rang out from his suggestion.

Nikkita straightened up with her tennis bat. "Let's?"

Ian spread his hands out at his sides. "In the spirit of a walk down memory lane," he proposed, starting to move in Nikkita's direction, and it occurred to her that he couldn't have a glove or ball with him anymore as his hands came inward to find their parking spaces.

He paused mid-step, giving Nikkita a significant look, his tone softening when he spoke again. "Our place is still there, you know."

The warm twinge that went through Nikkita's middle might have been one of surprise. Or delight.

Or homesickness.

"Is it?" she asked, buying time for her twinge.

Ian shuffled his feet like a hopeless nostalgic exposed. "It was a no-brainer for me to check for it when you said you'd swing by here." He hunched his shoulders somewhat for a further confession. "I even checked the menu online. In case you might want to go and..." He ducked his head and peeked over at her. "Order in order with me?"

That must have been the cue Nikkita's stomach needed to growl. Whether it was her physical stomach, however, or something deeper than that, giving off a craving signal, she wasn't sure.

The two of them took their cars on the special drive necessary to get them to their following destination. Upon their arrival inside, they chose to sit together in a booth, and once their order for lunch was on the table before them, Ian, to the tune of an oldies hit playing above their heads, picked up a diagonal half of a grilled cheese sandwich.

"Here's to faith," he said, holding the sandwich toward Nikkita beside him.

She also picked up half of her sandwich, dipped a corner of it into her tomato soup, and raised it up. "Here's to hope."

Ian gave his sandwich a belated dip in his own soup, lifting a reminding finger with his other hand. "And hope not to go home hungry."

"Bingo," Nikkita agreed, about to go in for the toast but stopping herself. "That is"—she sat up straighter to make a decorous correction—"amen."

Ian grinned at her. "Amen."

The two of them bumped knuckles in a toast with their sandwich hands and took the first bites into their lunch.

After the soup, sandwiches, and conversation over that course, they didn't need to consult the ice cream parlor's menu to discuss their next step.

"Two black and whites?" Ian checked with Nikkita.

"Hmm." She dabbed at her mouth with a napkin. "How about if we do something else today? Say, two brown cows." Thinking twice about that, she snapped her fingers. "Or double chocolate malts."

"Do something else?" Ian's head came to a doubtful slant. "See, now you're veering off memory lane."

"Am not." Nikkita indicated the establishment in general with its currently small crowd. "We didn't have black and whites every time we came here."

"No, but we did the first time," Ian almost interrupted her, teasing her, even if his hurry was too earnest to only have teasing in it. "The first time is what we're memory laning at the moment."

Something bashful crept into his look, and Nikkita couldn't laugh in response to it. She could smile, but she couldn't laugh. "Oh? Then why aren't we sitting up there at the counter, closer to the fountain action?"

Ian scooted closer to her on their shared seat. "Cozier in a booth."

She gave him that one but didn't let him off the hook. "And what about the jacket? If we're first-timing here, you should've brought the jacket." When Ian said nothing to that, Nikkita leaned toward him in confidential fashion, their shoulders bumping. "Do you still have the jacket?"

Ian averted his deadpan gaze away from her. "Doesn't fit anymore." Nikkita's hand flew up near her mouth in a halfhearted attempt to hide a chortle, and Ian came to his own defense. "I mean, I could get into it okay, last time I tried. But now I'd probably look a little more like a giant marshmallow than not if I tried to, uh..." He threw a furtive glance around them, resorting to a mumble. "Zip it up."

Nikkita let a fuller laugh loose, but it was one of comfortable empathy, her own changes in weight being able to relate. "Well, then, you see?" She reached around Ian, patting him on the back. "This lane is already different as it is. Why don't we keep on veering and be adventurous?" When he only pulled a feigned face at her, she said, "Hey, don't tell me you've given up your daredevil ways." She drummed her fingers down on the table with her free hand. "Not that a double chocolate malt is so daring of an extra step when you're already a guy sitting in an ice cream shop that's now officially a relic from last century. But, still."

As Ian peered down at her hand on the table, he brought his own hand over, warmly covering hers. "You're sitting right here in this relic with me," he told her, cracking a smile as their eyes met. "So don't sound so snooty."

The effort she took to produce a smirk wasn't the strongest one, what with the way her pulse took off in a diverting tap dance as Ian's fingers closed around hers. She relied on her voice to take up the jocular slack for her lips just then. "My fault," she said without a drop of remorse.

Ian was still holding Nikkita's hand when their server came over to take their dessert order. "Burn One All the Way," Ian delivered a hearty request. "For each of us, please."

Once their malts arrived, Ian let Nikkita's hand go and picked up his glass, holding it toward hers. She lifted her malt in full anticipation of his toast—

"And here's to love," he pronounced, giving Nikkita pause in spite of her anticipation, but the pause wasn't awkward in nature.

She and Ian stared at each other, their glasses in the air, past and present, difference and sameness blending together in their mutual space, seen and unseen, between and around them.

Ian had made the pronouncement, old and new at once. Accordingly, Nikkita supplied the conclusion for both aspects of it, feeling all of it.

She couldn't smile with her response, but she could feel.

"The greatest of these," Nikkita murmured, and she and Ian, after clinking their glasses together, took the first sips of their malts.

Amen.

After lunch, Ian invited Nikkita to follow him over to his house to get a look around the place. It didn't escape her notice that he said nothing about the house's location before they got into their cars, and the route she followed him on was too familiar for her not to be suspicious.

By the time they pulled up in the driveway of the Everson residence where Nikkita had frequently made herself at home in the past, her curiosity was duly piqued.

"So, I take it you're wondering why we're here," Ian stated the obvious once Nikkita came and joined him on the front stoop.

"Maybe. Kind of." She shrugged. "Kind of a lot."

Ian fiddled with the set of keys in his hand, picking out the right pair. "Well, they haven't made any official announcements yet," he began, bringing up one finger to tap against his lips, "but my mom is away on a honeymoon right now."

Nikkita's eyebrows climbed upward. "Is she?"

"She is. Eloped with one of her traveling buddies, and she's already got her important stuff moved over to his place." Ian used his keys in the front door's pair of locks. "So I'll be moving back here soon." He opened the door wide. "My house."

Neither of them stepped over the threshold. "Putting your other house up for sale?" Nikkita asked him.

Ian shook his head. "Going to rent it out. I already know this winning personality of mine works for home sales," he declared, giving his brows a waggle. "I figure potential tenants won't be able to resist me either."

"Wow. So you figure." Nikkita's head came to an affected tilt. "And to think I once had the nerve to call you 'humble.'"

Ian leaned, raising one arm and resting it against the doorjamb. "You have all the nerve in the world. Because you didn't just call me that. You sang it to me." A rakish smile of accusation stole across his face. "Played with my emotions."

Nikkita's lips formed a saucy pooch as she surveyed him, then she said, "Begging to differ. I didn't play with anything." Stepping close to him, she ran her eyes over the smear of her makeup still visible on his shirt, which he'd worn proudly all through lunch. "I played *on* your emotions," she told him, "and music came out." She reached up to take either side of his open collar in her hands, staring his accusation down with a smile of her own. "Word on the street is that I'm a musician."

Ian didn't have to move for something in the space between them, around them, to stir into subtle motion. "Yes. You are," he said, his eyelids lowering a degree, his gaze sweeping over Nikkita's face, making a swift drop to her mouth.

Nikkita allowed that bit of exchange its moment in time before she broke from it, taking it upon herself to pop Ian's collar in honor of them both.

Once the two of them were in the house, Nikkita was game to let Ian show her around as if she'd never been there before. She voiced her notice or admiration for some of the changes in paint, appliances, and furniture since she'd last been there. One room that hadn't changed much, however, was the last one they visited, and Nikkita took her usual step of respect into the den.

While Ian didn't pop a *Beaver* DVD into the player under the television, he and Nikkita did relax into the side-by-side armchairs in front of the closed armoire. They sat there in the presence of books and wood and leather and family essence, drinking in the atmosphere.

"Now," Ian spoke up, "doesn't this beat the two of us being polite and weird over the internet?"

Giving her eyes a good-natured roll, Nikkita looked over at Ian. "Have we really been that weird?"

"Um, no. Guess not. But we still weren't quite right, though. You know?"

Nikkita didn't deny that. She lowered her eyes to watch her hand smooth over the leather upholstery under it. "Speaking of the internet... To be honest, for some years there, I was waiting to see when you'd start posting about kids." She raised her gaze back to Ian. "You and Kelsey's."

He let out a short breath, giving Nikkita a half-smile. "No surprise there. You weren't the only one." He shrugged a shoulder. "It's people's natural expectation of young and youngish married couples, but Kelsey and I stayed child-free on purpose. And not only because we knew that carrying a child and putting Kelsey's body through childbirth might be too hard on her."

Ian rolled his head on the back of his chair, staring ahead of him, his smile lingering. "She was Kelsey Nightingale in her own right. A warrior too. Visiting kids in hospitals. Writing up petitions for our hospital district. Managing fundraisers. Championing the cause of research and cures for childhood diseases. She said she didn't feel like she was personally missing something or not doing enough by not having a child at home." His smile grew as he took his voice up a few octaves. "'The kids I meet and play and talk with all the time are like my angels. Even the imps.'"

Nikkita also smiled a little at that, and she waited to see if Ian was finished before she ventured to ask, "Did you feel the same way? Like nothing was missing for you personally?"

Ian turned his face back to Nikkita, snickering. "Make no mistake—I get pretty busy spoiling my nieces and nephews as much as my sister will let me, and they love getting in Uncle Ian's hair." He poked his tongue out of one side of his mouth and tousled himself somewhat about the head, drawing a titter out of Nikkita. "When the kids are done, I'm good with leaving them back in the care of their parents until the next time," he said, growing thoughtful. "I believe part of what made me and Kelsey right for each other is that I never felt like she and I were any less of a married couple or any less of a family than couples that have kids." He ran a tidying hand down the side and back of his hair. "Being family with her was different, yes. But not less."

His assertion held no lack of confidence, but he appeared hesitant afterward, as if trying to determine the likelihood of stepping on a toe or two of Nikkita's. "You, um, ever think about having kids? Of your own?" he asked.

A miniature laugh rippled from her at his question. "Who doesn't at least think about it at some point or another?" Her toes stayed right where they were, unbothered. "But as a single woman who's been living her passion, often on the road, I'm pretty sure I haven't thought about motherhood nearly as much as some people think all women do."

"Ah." Ian's hands opened and ballooned outward. "And you've still got a lot of family."

"*Oh* yes." Nikkita bounced with pleasure in her seat. "Now with my cousins having kids, it's been cousins, cousins galore when I make my visits."

The two of them bounded through talk of their extended families for a while, which led to Ian telling her, "Maybe needless to say, family became all the more important to me after my dad died. So I think it's only natural that I work helping people see their dream homes come to life." His fingers sketched out a general outline of a house before him. "Granted, a house, a building, isn't a home by itself. But when you create that space for people and their families and friends to *be*, and to be home to each other, to make memories together... Introducing them to their finished houses blows me away every time." He looked around the den with reflective eyes. "There's just something about being home."

There. It was too easy. An opening for Nikkita to express her understanding of his sentiments. An opening too easy for her to miss taking, or to miss taking it in song.

An oldie, of sorts.

"Ian Evvv-ver-son hummm-ble, there's noo-o place..."

Ian's eyes stopped where they were, took a minute to close, and then they came shining their way to Nikkita's. "See?" he asked. "See how much you inspired me in my life's work?" She was on the brink of responding with humor when he said, "I'm actually serious," halting her humor before it surfaced. "When I got into my career, you better believe I thought of you."

Nikkita didn't look around the room as he had, but she felt its essence all the more. Of course this den would be the place he'd tell her that.

"You didn't make me feel like a loser or anything when I was scared about the future," Ian pointed out. "I knew you believed in me."

A singular memory came to her in the form of music turned down low. In the remembrance of warm vanilla beneath her fingertips. In a sense of safety she'd once thought improbable, then thought it to be permanently lost.

"Yeah?" she whispered now, the corner of her mouth shaky in its lifting, though not because the emotion behind it wanted for anything.

After letting his clear appreciation rest untouched for a time, Ian cut a slice out of the humor he'd halted. "A girl wouldn't clap and yip and hoot around for me and almost scream out 'Ian Bean!' in a crowd of people if she didn't believe in me at least a little bit."

Nikkita had no problem lending a laugh to that, and she felt free to meet him in the same vein of sharing. "I've thought of you in my work too. Thought about the days I used to let you in on my music time." She nodded in the direction of the house's driveway. "Thought of you when I got Rosa."

Ian's attention followed her nod. "Your guitar."

"Mm hm. My manifest heartstrings," Nikkita affirmed. "She was a Christmas gift from my parents. I told them that being away from home made me want to learn a new instrument I could hold, like a close friend." Her arms embraced the invisible body of a smooth, curvaceous, mellow creation with a voice that needed Nikkita's hands for release. "She's so gorgeous, she made me remember the day of my first big stage. At the amphitheater."

Her mention of that momentous performance made Ian squint in thought until he recalled aloud, "When I gave you…"

"Roses. From the family." Nikkita's head inclined in Ian's direction. "You picked the color. Something different from the norm. Something you thought was appropriate. I wanted to always carry the heart of that day with me when I create and share music." Her embrace became another imaginary strum at strings, the rising glow of a smile bringing sunlight to the gray skies of her eyes. "Rosa."

That key collection of details seemed to amaze Ian to hear, but it wasn't only like a sense of surprise. An amazed kind of hope came glistening over the horizon in his face.

Nikkita remained aware of the horizon as she said, "Since the day I got her, she's been with me through thick and thin."

Ian sat forward in his chair, resting his elbows near his knees. Perhaps trying to steady himself or hold something in place. "I take it that this is thick? Being on tour?"

"It is. Maybe a little thin too, this time," Nikkita came right out and admitted, "since I don't know when I'll be touring again after this one wraps up."

It was apparent that Ian hadn't been expecting that bittersweet answer.

Nikkita went on to explain, "It's taken a lot for me to find the right fit of people to perform with. Not only for their technical talent but for their character. People I really vibe with and who vibe with each other on another level. People I like traveling with and who I can trust with my music. I've come too far to go touring with just anybody."

She gave a sigh, resigned and wistful. "A couple of my band members have decided to step back from touring and all to turn more focus on some personal stuff. And my drummer is about to switch career paths entirely. For the band in general, we decided to officially call our next step a hiatus." She waved her hand over the word as she might a bright title on a marquee. "But when it's pretty much indefinite, and you've got a hunch that you see more than 'hiatus' looming in your band's eyes while you're all working..."

"...Oh." Ian didn't presume to tack any more than that onto the end of her incomplete thought.

Nikkita turned her mind's eye away from the marquee. "Tough as it can be not having someone else drive you around on the road, I brought my own car this time. In case after our last stop, I'd want to just keep on driving." Not liking the almost morbid sound to the way she said that, she hurried on to clarify, "For a while. To decompress. To sightsee and let some of my songwriting ideas marinate. Gather some new ideas too. Get footage for my vlog. All that."

"I see. It sounds refreshing." Ian's knees were stirring from one side to the other, and he slowly rubbed his hands together. "In case you wouldn't have thought of adding it to your plans, you'd be welcome to stop by here again, sometime." His hands and knees went still. "Anytime."

Nikkita went still with him, recognizing so much relevant truth before her eyes. Ian was trying to keep steady, to hold hope in place, though it had already risen over the horizon.

He'd doubted that she trusted him enough to come back here. "For a visit," he'd been so careful to insert. Yet, it took no strain or struggle on her part to see that he, sitting there so steady, wanted more than another visit.

Nikkita raised a glass she wasn't presently holding. "Here's to love?" she inquired with a thickening voice.

Ian's mouth opened, his lips accompanied by an unspoken reply. Unspoken, but not unheard.

Nikkita shook her head in a positive sense. "It's so incredible," she said, a sudden, watery laugh escaping her without an outward smile. "It seemed like I wasn't going to do more than visit once, back when Jayme invited me to that Outreach Nite and introduced me like a pet she'd brought along from a foreign country. I went wandering around the church and thought about skipping the youth group service. That's when I found pre-service prayer."

Much as it had happened those years before, a part of Nikkita stole away from the room she was sitting in, going back to wait, to wonder, and to rest in a certain chapel, unhindered by the fact that the physical place no longer existed.

"I'd never been in an atmosphere like it," she said. "A presence like it. Before that, I guess I'd always thought of prayer as 'Now I lay me down to sleep,' but that wasn't what happened in the chapel. I couldn't even say exactly how it was that I encountered God, but He met me in that room. Something in me could tell, then and there, that I was…I was loved. Loved in a way I couldn't wrap my mind around, and it didn't feel like I had to." Her hand went up to sit at the base of her throat as she took in an enlivening breath. "I couldn't describe it, but it was real."

Ian's eyelids flickered as if that same breath, a wind, had come his way as well.

Nikkita's hand slid away from her throat. "Even though so much about my church experience there ended up getting destroyed, and then I slogged through questioning what was true and half-true and what was all a lie—still. It didn't change what had happened in that chapel." One of her arms folded over the other as she embodied an embrace of another kind. "Love got a hold of me that day, and He's held me ever since. I don't know what or where I'd be if He hadn't."

Ian made a low sound of concurrence, his hands again rubbing together. "Same."

Nikkita gave her arm an absent squeeze. "I'll never think it's less than egregious that to protect myself, I had to escape a church, of all places. It's just as bad whenever I hear stories from other people, about them having to do the same thing. So, the more I thought about it during counseling, the more I wondered how hollow or delusional it might sound to my parents, to tell them love met me at church." She wrinkled her nose, altering her voice. "'At *that* church? Where the people preaching on love and truth didn't even believe in it?'"

Ian sat up with a look of keen interest. "What'd you wind up telling them? Or did you tell them anything?"

Nikkita's arms eased downward, relaxing. "It was my mom who wound up telling *me* something, after I released my second album." The corners of her lips eased upward. "'Your father and I... Sometimes when we're listening, we hear God in your music, baby.'" At her disclosure, a spark of awe came to Ian's eyes, and Nikkita told him, "His love isn't restricted, and this journey isn't over."

It heartened her to hear that assurance come from her own mouth, like the closing line of grace from a soothing chorus.

And amen.

As the day slipped into late afternoon, Nikkita reluctantly told Ian it was time for her to be on her way. She'd have to get to her next destination for some rest and to "make sure my cords are clear of malt" for tomorrow night.

Ian, with his hands parked in his pockets, walked her out to her crossover in the driveway. As she opened her door to put her tote inside, he told her, "For the record, I wasn't trying to guilt you into coming here when I said I miss us."

Nikkita hadn't thought so. Did she need to say so? She turned to face Ian from around her door as he continued.

"I just thought if you would come, and if it'd be at all possible for us to go back and dig through some of what was then to help us see where we are now..." He brought his shoulders up. "Then we could go from here? However that would look for us."

Nikkita stared at him. However it would look?

Five or ten years out from now, it won't be just you.

A good deal more than either of those lengths of time had gone by, but Nikkita still saw what she'd seen back then. Only now she had a better, more seasoned idea of the way it looked, not limited or prevented by the passing of five or ten or—

"Yes," Ian said, now moving in so close that anyone watching him might have thought he also planned on getting into Nikkita's vehicle, "the love that got a hold of you back then was real." He brought his hands out of his pockets. "And so were we."

Even with all the remembering Nikkita had done since that morning, if someone were to ask her at that second what day it was and why she and Ian were standing outside, she would have found she'd forgotten.

Ian shook his head without taking his eyes from hers. "You weren't wrong that time you said most high school friendships don't last forever. But that's not all we were." He reached to take one of her hands in his. "That's why, yes, you're still in here," he testified, bringing her hand up, pressing it to the place she'd claimed on his chest.

She cherished the beating beneath her hand, the rhythm of flowing life making further testimony against her touch.

However it would look, he'd said. Oh, how nice.

Ian was being courteous and reserved about it. Giving her space to decline if she happened not to share his vision.

But he had as full a view of it as she did. Gazing up into his dark eyes brimming with the fervor of truth, Nikkita saw that Ian saw.

He was only leaving space for her to make a choice.

Several heartbeats later, after Nikkita had lifted her free hand to go around the back of Ian's neck and to guide his head downward, his quiet laughter was likely a sign that he hadn't anticipated her lips brushing a trail of affection over his bean speckles.

Nonetheless, he must not have been taken too far off guard, given that he had the presence of mind to nudge a detour into Nikkita's trail. What a day for detours this was, and she had no regrets about either: the one she'd taken to swing by this town, or the one she now followed in order to fall all the way into the past multiplying within the present.

Here's to love.

It was a toast unlike any other. Sameness and newness blended together in their mutual space as Nikkita and Ian brought their lips together, taking the first taste of their first kiss.

It wasn't a first like that of inexperienced youth, however. Ian wasted little time in clearing the two of them of the crossover door that was in their way, leaving the claim on his chest to Nikkita so that he could draw her firmly against him with both his hands around her waist.

The first taste melted into a second. Then deepened into a third. Nikkita kept a secure hold on Ian's nape as she opened her mouth with as much passion as she ever did to sing, and in their pause from the technicalities of passing time between and around them, the two of them commenced making their own style of music.

Pleasing and intense. Pure and true.

Chapter Eleven

FOR NOW, IT WAS NIKKITA and Rosa alone at center stage, Nikkita sitting on a stool with Rosa in her lap, each of them with their own mic to amplify their voices for this creation of soulful verses with a chorus.

It wasn't the warmest of summer nights out here at the amphitheater, but Nikkita didn't feel any chill in her amethyst, off-shoulder jumpsuit with its subtle shimmer. She'd kept moving during most of her numbers, and perhaps even in winter, she wouldn't freeze here under the hot stage lights at such a concert.

Even so, the lights were down low now, keeping Nikkita as the stage's only focal point. Because she didn't need to have her in-ear monitors in while Rosa was the only instrument serving to accompany her, Nikkita could take some time settling into a deeper connection with her large listening audience.

Then, it was back to connecting with her band members as they gradually joined her once she reached the bridge.

Our silence was golden,
but forever treasures are chosen.
The words urge us to catch them,
to find they're diamonds and platinum...

The lights brought more illumination onstage as the song rounded a bend and made an unrushed escalation in energy. In light of this being one of Nikkita's most popular songs, along with the high odds that this would be the last time this specific group of performers would ever perform it all together, they gave themselves up to their accord and instrumentation as far as they pleased, letting the song ride while the riding was fire.

Your heartstrings,
my everything—
we're ready.
My love, let's play...

The group of ardent artists onstage played on.

At length, Nikkita stood up, a stagehand coming and removing the stool for her as she went over to set Rosa on her guitar stand and to take a needed swig from a bottle of water. Emotion was ready to rise in her throat, and all these years later, she still wouldn't want to embarrass the memory of her Renée by going croaky in front of an audience.

Nikkita signaled for the band to keep riding but at a lower level, and she returned to her mic, adjusting the stand.

"Hey there," she addressed her audience, again removing her monitors from her ears. "Do you all know how great you've been tonight? Magnificent." She waited through their responding flow of cheers, then told them, "I almost hate to wrap up this experience we've had. I really do. But I know you're more than ready to go all out with me for one more song, yeah?"

More cheering, and Nikkita directed her own brief round of applause to the audience.

"Before we go there," she went on, "I want to take a quick minute to thank a source of inspiration of mine, who wound up making this trip a homecoming for me." She lifted her hands to block the stage lights from her eyes and peered into the audience as if she could see everyone's faces.

"Humble bumblebee boo-boo?" Nikkita called out. "You know who you are. Come on down." As a questioning hum rolled through the audience, Nikkita smirked. "Don't worry, boo-boo. Security was already expecting you." She gave a laugh meant only for his ears, regardless of the amphitheater in general being able to hear her anyway. "I won't have them kick you out."

It didn't take too long before Nikkita could make out a recognizable figure a short way off, approaching down an aisle. The sides of his spruce, classic sports jacket were hiked up a tad where his hands were parked in their usual spaces in a pair of dark jeans, his stride as casual as anything while he came in answer to Nikkita's summons.

Sure, she'd be seeing him soon at an after-party with her band that night, but there wouldn't be as many people at the party to witness this. She figured that he, along with her return to this big stage, deserved a grand gesture to set up the finale.

Given the stage's physical height, Nikkita had to move forward and kneel on the edge of it to come closer to face level with Ian once he'd made it there.

"Seriously, Nikki?" he asked with a grin as Nikkita leaned to hear him amid the riding music and the rising hum of interest from the audience. "Extreme mush in the mic? In front of the whole world?" Though he seemed helpless to hide the pleasure and pride in his grin, he narrowed his eyes. "I'll get you for this."

Nikkita reached to place a hand on his cheek, smiling down into those eyes. "You don't have to get me, Bean." She brought her mouth close to his ear. "You already have me." With that, she pulled back just enough to see the glistening of hope coming into realization in his gaze.

Along her ongoing journey of creating and sharing, she'd have plenty of time to write and sing one of her many songs to him, whether or not the specific one now awakening in her mind would end up on her vlog or her next album for the rest of the world to listen to.

A song about Ian's heart: her dream home.

For the time being, it more than sufficed that the vibing band members onstage knew how to catch an undirected cue, taking the music up to the level of an eloquent anthem, and the animated sound of acclamation rose from the audience as Nikkita Creighton indulged in a public display of affection with the man she'd called out from the crowd.

Their kiss might not have been of the same blazing nature as those Nikkita and Ian shared the day before. That would have been much to indulge in before such an audience. But tonight's kiss was still warm. Rich. Equally true.

And through the amphitheater's atmosphere, the music played on: all that was within, beneath, and around it. Even more beyond it, with vitality like the verses and refrain of a sacred hymn, or like the blast and flow of jazz and soul, or like the bopping and crooning of a time-honored oldie that would never grow old—a collective essence riding the air, still profound even when love transcended description, and when its lyrics, for a space in time, went unsung.

Unsung, in a literal way. But no less real.

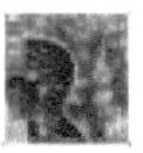

A glorious reunion.
An early gift.
A new season of love.

Don't miss the holiday sequel to *We Were Real*,
A Christmas So Real

An abuse survivor shares reflections to raise Christians' awareness, discussing some key ways in which abuse finds a place in churches, and expressing thoughts on how to combat this issue—an issue Christianity can't afford to ignore.

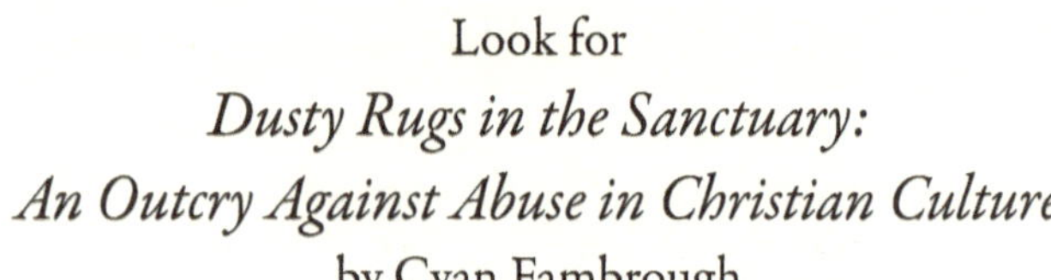

Look for
Dusty Rugs in the Sanctuary:
An Outcry Against Abuse in Christian Culture
by Cyan Fambrough

To find all of Nadine's books and her blog featuring book reviews as well as posts on writing, diversity, films, and more, visit:

www.prismaticprospects.wordpress.com

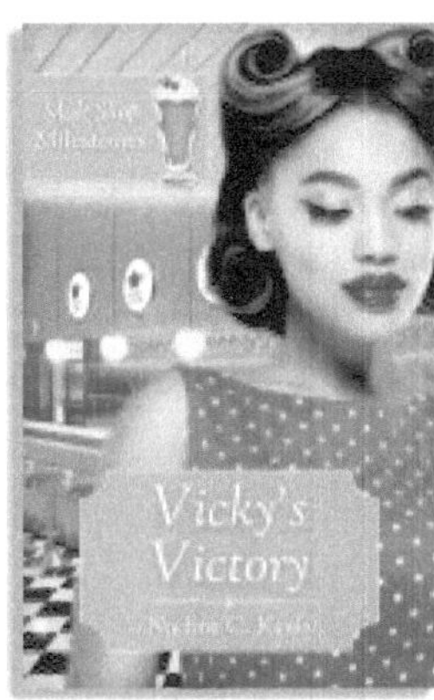